MARRYING A COWBOY

CALLAHANS OF COPPER CREEK BOOK 8

NATALIE DEAN

DEDICATION

I'd like to dedicate this book to YOU! All of my wonderful readers that have been following my stories over the years.

We're embarking on another new journey through Copper Creek. I hope you enjoy these stories as much as you've loved the Baker brothers!

Thank you to my biggest fans.... There's a lot of you! Jess, Bernie, Wren, Judy, Sherry, Vicci, Phyllis, Debbie, Indra, Jennifer, Carol, Jeanette, Margaret, Paul, and I know there's more I didn't list. But thank you all!

And I can't leave out my wonderful mother, son, sister, and Auntie. I love you all, and thank you for helping me make this happen.

Most of all, I thank God for blessing me on this endeavor.

AND... I've got a special team of advance readers who are always so helpful in pointing out any last minute corrections that need to be made. I'm so thankful to those of you who are so helpful!

ALSO BY NATALIE DEAN

CONTEMPORARY ROMANCE

Copper Creek Romances

BAKER BROTHERS OF COPPER CREEK

Copper Creek Romances Series 1

Cowboys & Protective Ways

Cowboys & Crushes

Cowboys & Christmas Kisses

Cowboys & Broken Hearts

Cowboys & Second Chances

Cowboys & Wedding Woes

Cowboys' Mom Finds Love

CALLAHANS OF COPPER CREEK

Copper Creek Romances Series 2

Making a Cowgirl

Marrying a Cowgirl

Christmas with a Cowgirl

Trusting a Cowgirl

Dating a Cowgirl

Catching a Cowgirl

Loving a Cowgirl

Marrying a Cowboy

KEAGANS OF COPPER CREEK

Copper Creek Romances Series 3

Some Cowboys are Off-Limits

Some Cowgirls Love Single Dads

Some Cowboys are Infuriating

Some Cowboys Don't Like City Girls

Some Cowboys Heal Broken Hearts

Some Cowgirls are Worth Protecting

Some Cowboys are Just Friends

Some Cowboys Fall for Hidden Stars

Some Cowboys Come Home for Christmas

Some Cowboys Brave the Flames

Some Cowboys Fight for Love

PALMERS OF COPPER CREEK

Copper Creek Romances Series 4

Mateo & Nicole

Sophia & Cameron

Roman & Olivia

Camilla & Dallas

Isabelle & Jason

Marcus & Wynter

Miller Family Saga

BROTHERS OF MILLER RANCH

Miller Family Saga Series 1

Her Second Chance Cowboy

Saving Her Cowboy

Her Rival Cowboy

Her Fake-Fiance Cowboy Protector

Taming Her Cowboy Billionaire

BROTHERS OF MILLER RANCH SERIES BUNDLE

MILLER BROTHERS OF TEXAS

Miller Family Saga Series 2

The New Cowboy at Miller Ranch

Humbling Her Cowboy

In Debt to the Cowboy

The Cowboy Falls for the Veterinarian

Almost Fired by the Cowboy

Faking a Date with Her Cowboy Boss

MILLER BROTHERS OF TEXAS SERIES BUNDLE

BRIDES OF MILLER RANCH, N.M.

Miller Family Saga Series 3

Cowgirl Fallin' for the Single Dad

Cowgirl Fallin' for the Ranch Hand

Cowgirl Fallin' for the Neighbor

Cowgirl Fallin' for the Miller Brother

Cowgirl Fallin' for Her Best Friend's Brother

Cowboy Fallin' in Love Again

BRIDES OF MILLER RANCH, N.M. SERIES BUNDLE

Though I try to keep this list updated in each book, you may also visit my website nataliedeanbooks.com for the most up to date information on my book list.

CONTENTS

1

———

One more to go.

Technically, Zeke didn't have to worry anymore. Eloise was his last daughter to be married and that would happen soon enough. Each of his daughters had found someone he could tolerate. Sure, some of these men were better than others, but his daughters were happy and that was all that mattered.

Right?

Of course it was. His late wife would be turning in her grave if she heard even a whiff of uncertainty on his part. That was something he'd figured out over the more recent years. His daughters needed room to spread their wings as much as he hated to let them do it.

That was why he'd retreated out to his hunting cabin on the edge of the forest. The more time he spent under his own roof, the harder it was to mind his own business.

Brielle had nearly driven him to distraction with the two

young men who came and went. It was much smarter to be out here where there was only one bedroom, a living space, and a kitchen. It couldn't be more than five-hundred square feet, but it suited him just fine.

No women to disrupt his routine, and he was still close enough to the ranch that he could show up and get work done without anyone being the wiser. Zeke didn't even know if his daughters were aware he wasn't sleeping at home. They were all so caught up in their relationships, and he made a point to join them at mealtime.

Thunder cracked outside the hunting cabin and the building creaked along with the wind. The storm had moved in fast after Brielle's wedding was over. A weather warning had been sent out to the residents of Copper Creek for high winds and hail.

Zeke pulled off his boots and wandered toward the window to peer out into the darkness. There wasn't much he could see. Not even the swaying of the trees. The moon was completely shrouded in storm clouds and only the barest glow on the edges of objects gave his view depth.

The average person would see all this darkness and immediately get claustrophobic, but Zeke found he liked the never-ending darkness a lot more than the stark light of a typical day. He leaned his shoulder against the wall beside the window, relishing in the thunder and the sound of the hail hitting the house.

A bright flash of lightning zig-zagged through the sky and small tendrils of energy seemed to pour off it as it darted through the clouds. He could smell the electricity in the air and feel the hum of it as it fueled the nature that surrounded him.

Thunder boomed almost immediately after. The lightning had been close. He'd have to keep an eye on the woods surrounding his property in case it started a fire.

The storm continued to rage with more bursts of lightning. Then one slammed into the earth.

Zeke straightened, his eyes narrowing as he peered out the window and into the darkness. There was no way that bolt didn't do some damage. Most of the ones prior fizzled out before hitting anything, but that last one most definitely made contact.

His heart thumped with anticipation. The rain and hail had stopped, but the wind had picked up. That wasn't a good sign. The lightning storm was moving away, which meant more peace around here, but his gut was telling him that they were going to be dealing with the aftermath for days, if not weeks.

Shifting nervously, he raked a hand through his hair. He was still dressed in his suit and tie from the wedding, and if he'd had any sense, he would have changed right away. Now, it was too late. If there was, in fact, something he would have to deal with, he wouldn't have time to change. The winds alone would add problems to any fire that might have been started.

Still, he searched the horizon for the smallest hint that something was wrong.

Then he saw it.

It was barely discernable, but thanks to the blacked-out sky, he was able to see it.

A soft glow behind the line of trees to the east. That wasn't where his home was, thankfully. If he was lucky, it was just a field that had caught fire and all he'd have to do is call in some reinforcements to control the spread.

His brows lowered.

Actually, from this distance, the fire looked too far away to be on his property but only just. Zeke racked his brain for the folks who lived out in that direction. Ruth Mumford used to live out that way, but she'd since moved out of state to be closer to family.

His brows shot up. Last he'd heard, a family had moved in,

but he wasn't sure who. There had been a lot of turnover in town. Any of the new faces he interacted with could live there now.

Zeke darted from the window toward his boots. He yanked them on, his eyes flitting to the window as the glow grew stronger. It was a house. The house was on fire; he was certain of it. By the time he saddled his horse, the winds had died down, but the glow in the distance was still raging.

Praying he wasn't too late and that no one was harmed, he kicked his heels into his horse's flanks and darted into the night.

The path was familiar, easy to traverse even in the dark. Once upon a time he might have considered dating Miss Mumford. She'd lost her husband a few years after he'd lost his wife. But the timing had never been right. That didn't stop them from forming a friendship, and he'd visited her on occasion.

Smoke quickly inundated his senses the closer he got to the edge of his property. The glow burned brighter, and by the time the house appeared in his sights, he could hear the sirens, but they were too far away. The small house wasn't quite engulfed in flames, but it would definitely need to be rebuilt.

Zeke leaned forward in the saddle, urging his horse to move faster. Wind whipped at his face and tugged at his suit coat. He hadn't grabbed his hat, but if he had, it would have been long gone by now.

He arrived at the edge of the property and jumped from his saddle onto the ground. He sprinted toward the front entrance of the house and checked the knob, but it was locked. Pounding his fist against the wood, he hollered, "Hello! Is anyone in there?"

No sound came from within. The wind had now died down to a breeze, and the only thing he could hear was the crackling of wood being consumed by the flames.

"Hello!" he called again.

No answer, so he darted around the back of the house, but there was no way to get in. The strike must have originated from this side of the home. Once again, he charged around to the front, determined to ram his shoulder into the door. If he had to break the whole thing down, he'd do so just to make sure everyone was safe.

Zeke took the steps two at a time and braced himself before running at the door and slamming his shoulder into it.

Pain radiated from his shoulder and down his arm causing his fingers to tingle. Once again, he charged at the door, and this time he hit it in just the wrong place that something popped.

More pain shot through him, making him lose his breath. He gasped, seeing stars. "If anyone is here, you need to come out. There's a fire—"

"What in heaven's name are you doing?"

He whirled around and came face-to-face with a woman who looked vaguely familiar. They must have crossed paths at some point in town. Her blue eyes were bright and yet accusatory at the same time. Her hair was pulled away from her face, but it was too dark to tell if it was black or brown.

Zeke held his shoulder, shaking off his surprise. "Do you live here?"

She placed her hands on her hips. "Of course I live here." Her eyes shifted to the house and a sadness filled them. "Or at least I did. Do you mind getting off the porch so that the entire house doesn't just collapse on you? My son has already called for help. They'll be here any minute."

He lurched forward, doing as she said. "Was anyone hurt? That storm—"

"We're fine. As you can see, the damage was strictly to the house. I'm sorry, who are you?"

Ignoring her question, he nodded to the house. "Do you

have an extinguisher? Hose? Something we can use to put this out?"

"Like I said, there's nothing we can do. They'll be here soon." She glanced over her shoulder toward the horse. "Did you *ride* here? Do you live nearby?"

Zeke shot one more disgruntled look at the house, then shook his head. She was probably right. He moved to shake her hand, then winced as the pain of moving his arm nearly incapacitated him.

Her eyes dipped to where he held his shoulder, then lifted, and once again she set him with a disapproving stare. "You dislocated your shoulder."

"No, I probably just bruised it."

She moved toward him, shaking her head. "I've dealt with those kinds of injuries before. I know what I'm talking about. Your arm needs to be popped back into place. It's not going to feel great, but you should get immediate relief—"

"It's fine," he grunted as he shied away from her. Who did this woman think she was? "Are you even a doctor?"

Her smile momentarily threw him off guard. "No, but I was an athletic trainer back in Denver for the Broncos. You'd be surprised at the stuff I had to learn." She inched closer, her gaze still glued to his arm. "I promise it will only be a mild discomfort compared to what you're currently dealing with."

Again, he took a step away from her. The slightest movement was enough to set off a chain reaction of sharp pains that set his teeth on edge. Perhaps she made a good point. Whatever she might do couldn't be worse than what he felt at that moment.

Zeke let out a resigned sigh. "Fine. Make it quick."

"You're going to have to stay very still. I need the leverage to move it back into place."

He was just about to point out that she couldn't possibly

possess the strength to fix his shoulder when he heard a pop at the very same moment a howl escaped his lips.

She stepped back and offered him a patronizing sort of smile. "See? Now isn't that better?"

Zeke stared down at his shoulder with surprise. In his entire career, he'd never needed something like this to happen. And hopefully he wouldn't have to worry about it needing to be done ever again.

His arm felt hot and cold all at once, but the one thing that outshined all sensations was the relief this woman had promised. When his gaze flitted up to meet hers, she was smiling at him in a way that made him feel like an utter idiot.

Sirens blared beside them, bringing everything into focus. Zeke jumped back and retrieved his horse, then focused on staying out of the way.

The firemen made quick work of extinguishing the flames, leaving the building smoking. The woman stared forlornly at the building—her home. Zeke wasn't sure how long she'd been living at this residence, but it couldn't have been long. Still, this was a loss and one he couldn't help sympathizing with.

She spoke with the head of the fire department and he only caught snippets. Her last name was Birch. She was living here alone, but her son worked at a local ranch. She didn't have any family nearby.

Zeke inched closer, but he kept his focus trained on the building and the other firemen.

"There's no one you could stay with?" the fire chief asked, his eyes trained on the pad of paper in his hand. "It's better if you have a support system."

Ms. Birch shook her head. "I don't have any family. My parents passed away a few years ago, and Tom is my only son." Just as she mentioned his name, a cowboy came sprinting at her. "Good, it's out. I tried to track down Mr. Callahan, but he wasn't home."

Zeke stiffened and the familiar young man seemed to sense it. He glanced toward Zeke and his eyes widened.

"Mr. Callahan—what are you..." He shook his head, then turned to Ms. Birch. "I'll be right back." The young man hurried toward Zeke. "I'm sorry. What are you doing here?"

He gestured toward the smoking building. "I saw the fire from my hunting cabin." Tilting his head, he took in the young man. He looked familiar, but his daughters had done their own share of hiring over the last few months. Adeline was making the ranch more and more her own these days. "You work for me?"

"I'm Tom. Brielle hired me to be one of the tour guides at the ranch about two weeks ago." Tom held out his hand. "It's nice to finally meet you face-to-face, sir."

Zeke accepted the young man's firm grip and nodded. "You were looking for me?"

Tom started and glanced toward his mother. "Yes, I was going to see if there was space in the wrangler's quarters for my mother and I—just until we can find a place, of course. I wouldn't even ask, but..."

He could feel several pairs of eyes on him. His own shifted to Ms. Birch. "Absolutely not." Zeke crossed his arms and his eyes narrowed. "Under no circumstances will I allow that fine woman to bunk up with a bunch of wranglers."

Tom blinked. His uncertainty was almost humorous. "Sir?"

"You may stay in the bunkhouse, but your mother is welcome to use my hunting cabin." Zeke sensed more than watched Ms. Birch react. He couldn't tell if she was pleased with the offer or not.

Well, he didn't make the offer to please her. He did so because it was the right thing to do.

"Mr. Callahan, that is truly very generous of you, but—"

He turned toward her. "Do you have any other options?"

She didn't respond. This time, the onlookers were staring at her.

"Well? I think everyone here would like to know the answer to that question seeing as we've disrupted the flow of things around here."

To that statement some of the firemen jolted into action, leaving the chief, Tom, his mother, and Zeke. Ms. Birch shifted where she stood, her eyes darting from Zeke to her son and back. It was getting rather ridiculous—her waiting. The answer was simple. She needed a place, and he had one to offer. What was so hard about that?

2

———————

Agatha

How could this man not see just how hard it was for Agatha to accept his offer? He was a stranger. Even her son hadn't met him face-to-face before. She hadn't been thrilled about the notion of staying in the wrangler's quarters when Thomas had run off to ask, but she hadn't been able to stop him either.

At least staying with her son, she wouldn't feel like she was putting anyone out. The hunting cabin Mr. Callahan had offered wasn't ideal for a woman who was used to handling everything on her own.

She straightened her back and set a firm stare on this presumptuous man. "No, I don't have anywhere to stay at the moment. But I'm sure I can find accommodations—"

"And you have," Mr. Callahan stated as if he were discussing whether or not he wanted milk in his morning coffee. "I have offered you a place to stay, and you can accept it."

Agatha let out a strangled laugh. "We haven't even

discussed a rental rate, not to mention there's no telling how long it will take to rebuild."

"You're welcome to stay at that cabin for as long as you need, no charge."

She snapped her mouth shut, but doing so didn't stop her eyes from growing large. "I beg your pardon? I can't just—"

"You can and you will. I don't see any other option, do you? It's nearly midnight and everything in town is closed for the night."

Agatha scoffed. "Not everything."

"Unfortunately, he's right, ma'am," the chief cut in. He offered her an embarrassed smile. "If you don't have family or friends here, there are only a few other options. You stay at the station with us, or you drive into Colorado Springs. They'll have hotels that are open twenty-four-seven."

She blinked at him, then swung her focus to her son. "I haven't been in town much. Is he right?"

"Mom," he muttered. There was a hint of embarrassment in his voice. "I think the fire chief would know what he's talking about." Thomas gestured toward Mr. Callahan, someone whose reputation had preceded him when they'd moved to town.

Agatha hadn't been thrilled about Thomas working for the man after learning about his strict nature, but according to her son, he was the only one who paid decently. And she'd long since learned not to butt into her son's business.

She crossed her arms and tapped her foot. "I still don't see how you can expect me to just move into some stranger's home."

"It's not his home, Mom. He lives at the ranch. This is his hunting cabin." Thomas groaned and shot a wary glance at his boss. That was when it dawned on her that she was making a scene and he could get in trouble with the one person who helped them to pay their bills.

Agatha finally met Mr. Callahan's gaze. "You're sure it wouldn't put you out?"

Without wasting a moment, he said, "I wouldn't have offered if it would."

Thomas moved closer to her, his chin lowering just over her shoulder as he whispered, "Just thank the man and let's head out. We could use some sleep after the night we've had."

She shot him a disgusted look. No one bossed her around. She'd left that life when her ex-husband couldn't grasp the concept, and she'd never looked back. She didn't need anyone to take care of her, and she wasn't about to start now.

A glance at Mr. Callahan confirmed he was still staring at her, so she quickly schooled her features. She'd have a talk with her son about this in the morning after they took stock of the damage. Agatha nodded curtly toward Mr. Callahan. "Thank you for your generosity—"

He didn't even allow her to finish her thought as he climbed into his saddle and nodded toward Thomas. "Meet me at my place and I'll take you to the hunting cabin. It's only a few minutes' drive from the house."

He only winced once as he was adjusting himself in the saddle, and she knew his shoulder had to be killing him. But just like that, he dug his heels into his horse's sides and shot off into the dark.

Agatha snorted, shooting a look of disbelief at the fire chief. "Is he always like that?"

The man was staring down at his notebook and only glanced up at her for a moment. "Like what?"

"So bossy? I mean, I've heard the stories about his daughters... but does he think he can just tell everyone what to do?"

The chief lowered his pad of paper and a wry smile crossed his face. "You really must be new around here."

"We've only lived here a few months."

He nodded. "Sounds about right. Zeke Callahan is basically

Copper Creek royalty. He built his fortune and expanded his property by sheer will and through his blood, sweat, and tears. That man has earned the right to tell folks around here what to do."

She lifted a brow. "That sounds rather dangerous."

The chief shrugged. "I don't know. His family has ties to the founding members of this town, and he makes sure to help out where he can. Not a year goes by where he doesn't make a huge charitable contribution to the firemen's ball. If I remember right, he also pulled a few ranches from the edge of bankruptcy."

Words failed her in that moment. This wasn't what she'd expected at all. The Mr. Callahan she'd heard about was strict, tough, and hard on everyone he was supposed to love. Who in their right mind would require their eldest daughters to get married before the younger ones? They were living in a modern century, for crying out loud.

"Mom, let's go." Thomas tugged on her arm. "I don't know how long it will take Mr. Callahan to get back home, but it's already so late I don't think we should keep him waiting."

He was right, of course. She wouldn't have wanted to keep anyone up and waiting for her. But now that she had a bit more information on the man who had offered up his home, she knew she needed to show him proper respect.

Agatha reached out and touched the fire chief's forearm. "Thank you for your help tonight."

"All in a day's work, ma'am." He touched the brim of his helmet and strode toward his firetruck.

There wasn't anything of hers that she could gather. All she had were the clothes on her back. Thankfully, she'd opted to wear flannel pajama pants and a T-shirt. Otherwise, the inter-action with Mr. Callahan when he'd arrived would have been far more awkward.

She fidgeted in the passenger seat of her son's truck as she stared out into the dark expanse that was the country. They'd been city folk for so long that she'd almost forgotten what it was like living out here. There were nights when it was so quiet and so dark that her mind could play tricks on her. On more than one occasion, she'd been able to see things out her window she was sure weren't real.

It wasn't often, but when she found herself missing the city, it was usually the noises and the light. There was plenty to do, hear, and see in the city, which made living in a place like this incredibly dull.

But this was where Thomas wanted to live. He was far more interested in the ranching community than he'd let on, so she followed him. There was nothing left for her in the city, and a nice young man who did a lot of charity work had scooped her up, allowing her to have a job far quicker than she'd expected.

Shane would have to hear about the incident. For all she knew, he was already aware.

Agatha picked up her phone and stared at the screen as it lit up in the darkness.

"Expecting a call?" Thomas's soft voice flitted toward her.

"No."

The quiet filled the air between them. She could tell he was itching to ask her what she was doing looking at her phone this late at night. Heaving a sigh, she put the phone back on her seat. "I wonder if Shane heard about the fire."

"Why would he even be up?"

She shrugged. "That young man has his fingers in every-thing. I wouldn't be surprised if he bought out the local news-paper so he could control the narrative around his own company."

Thomas eyed her. "I thought you said he was a good guy and an even better boss."

"He's amazing. But he's also got a lot of money, and when a

man has expendable income, they tend to manipulate the world around them to best fit their agenda. No one is immune to that. Not even Shane."

Once again, he glanced at her out of the corner of his eye. "I don't know. From what I have heard, the people in town idolize folks like Shane and Zeke Callahan."

She rolled her eyes. "Don't get me started on what your boss has hiding in his closet. And you were the one who told me about most of it."

"Yeah? Well, maybe I was wrong. You heard what the chief said. Zeke Callahan might be protective, but at least he's protective of a lot more than just himself. He cares about the town too. Doesn't that make you like him just a little more?"

She shifted her gaze to the window in front of her, hands clasped even tighter in her lap. "I don't have to like him. He's not my boss. And as far as I'm concerned, I'm going to stay out of his hair. I'll touch base with the motel in the morning and see if they have any long-term options, and then I'll talk to Shane, too."

"You can't do that!"

She snorted. "Why not?"

"Because Zeke offered you an entire cabin to yourself. He's not even going to make you pay rent. All those firefighters heard him do so. If you turn that down, do you know what kind of reputation you would get?"

Once again, she let out an unladylike snort. "I don't really care what the town thinks of me. I'm not some simpering young woman who has to find a husband or risk losing everything she owns. We live in modern times, or have you forgotten that one little tidbit of information? I'm the one on the mortgage. I'm the one who has to file the insurance report. Me. I don't have to be accountable to anyone else in this world or any other for that matter."

The second she was done with her little speech, she sucked in a deep breath and let it out slowly. She wasn't overreacting. There was no such thing when she needed to provide for herself and the safety of her son. While the chief had allowed her to think of Mr. Callahan in a slightly better light, she wasn't about to allow the man to infiltrate her thoughts and change her behavior.

She was about set in her thoughts when they pulled up in front of the large ranch house. She'd seen brief glimpses of the Callahan property when she'd come to pick Thomas up a few hours ago, but she'd been distracted by the party. Now as she stared at the house through the truck window, she actually had a moment to reflect. When the chief had said royalty, he wasn't kidding. The house had an oversized porch wrapping clear around the whole thing. The paint was a classic white with accented shutters. Even in the dark, it looked impressive. If what she'd been told was true, then Mr. Callahan had built this whole place from the ground up, and he'd managed to keep it going despite raising seven girls all on his own.

She couldn't help but feel the slightest degree of awe for the man.

What was wrong with her that up until this moment, she'd still been insisting that she didn't need nor want to have anything to do with him? Clearly, this man had a lot more layers than he'd been letting on.

Just because rumors circulated around this man didn't mean that he was exactly what everyone said he was.

Agatha got out of the truck and stood beside it, her eyes still drinking in the property. It wasn't just the house that was impressive. He had several structures on the premises. There were at least two barns she could see in the distance. Then again, one might be something else. The property spread farther than her own, and she'd thought she'd lucked out when she bought the land from the previous owner.

"See? Didn't I tell you that Mr. Callahan's property was impressive? You only got to see the barn up close. It's different when you're *here*."

She shot a look at her son out of the corner of her eye, not wanting to admit to him that she had been thinking something similar.

"And you're not even seeing it in the day. When you came earlier, it was getting darker. Just wait until you see the sun come up over the horizon."

"It's still just a house," she murmured. "And frankly, I'm beginning to miss ours already despite how much smaller it is."

Thomas chuckled. "You'll see what I mean when you get to take a real tour of the place." There was awe in his voice as his gaze swept over the large house. She could see it in his eyes; he looked up to this man. But he barely knew the guy. How could he assume that Callahan was any better than the rest of them?

Agatha turned toward her son and took his hands in hers. She set her steely eyes on him, praying he would understand what she was about to say. "Having things... having power... it is all for nothing if you don't have someone to share it with. One day you will find someone to share your life with, and it won't matter if you live on a grand estate or in a tiny apartment. What will matter is the love you share with one another."

Tom's eyes dropped down to meet hers and he frowned. She could almost predict what was going to come out of his mouth next. "But you didn't have that with Dad."

She shook her head. "No, I didn't. I thought I did when we were first married, but he changed." Agatha reached up and pressed her hand to the side of her son's face. "But now I have you and that's all I need."

"Don't you ever... I dunno... wish things were different?"

She laughed. "There's nothing I could ever want more than what I have now." Agatha grimaced. "Well, perhaps a house that wasn't struck by lightning."

A deep voice sounded out in the darkness. "Ah, you've made it. Right, then, let me show you to your quarters."

Together, Agatha and Thomas turned toward the intrusion, finding Zeke standing with his arms crossed just a few yards away. She pulled away from her son and offered him a reassuring smile. "Shall we?"

3

———

Zeke

The whole ride back to the ranch, Zeke's thoughts got away from him. This woman and her son were new to the area, and while he was certain he had crossed paths with her before, he still couldn't place her.

Zeke knew everyone in town.

At least he used to.

He'd taken it upon himself a long time ago to meet everyone who moved in so he could size them up and make sure they weren't a threat to his livelihood.

Had he gotten so off course with his daughters that he'd dropped the ball on this one? How many more people had moved into the small town that he wasn't aware of? There had to be several now that Shane's equine therapy business had drawn the attention of the wealthier people in the state. Folks were using this place as a getaway from their city life, and while they weren't permanent residents, they were still here.

He was losing his grasp on the fortress that was Copper Creek.

His eyes darted from Ms. Birch to Tom. Neither one of them had presented a concern about any other family members in the area. That meant that this Ms. Birch might not have a husband.

Zeke shied away from that intrusive thought. He had no business wondering about her private life. She would be his guest, nothing more.

But as such, he would place her under the same protection he would any other visiting member of the community. There were dangerous animals out in the back part of his property—a wildlife he was content to let roam as long as it didn't interfere with the safety of his cattle.

He jerked his chin toward the barn. "The bunk house is on the other side of the barn. Tom knows where it is. I've already given the men the heads-up that you're coming."

The two individuals standing before him glanced at one another. He couldn't tell if they were actually worried about splitting up or if their hesitation was something else.

Either way, he wasn't in the mood for waiting. He had to get a few things squared away back at the cabin. Time was already short. "Well? Get on with it, then."

Tom lunged forward with a sharp nod. "Yes, sir. Thank you." The young man moved past him with sure, quick steps, and Zeke turned to Ms. Birch.

"Come along, then. We have a little bit of a ride to get out to the cabin."

"A ride?" she sputtered. "You can't honestly be suggesting that we ride horses out in the middle of the night."

He stopped and gave her a funny look. Wasn't he on a horse already this evening? That was beside the point. "No, we won't be riding horses. I have an ATV we'll take. It's something we can both ride together, and it might be faster, considering your fear of horses."

She stiffened. "I'm not afraid of horses."

"You sure seem anxious about getting into the saddle."

Her mouth snapped shut and she crossed her arms.

Zeke bit back a chuckle. "So you weren't just expressing your displeasure over riding a horse a few minutes ago?"

"I expressed my displeasure of riding a horse in the middle of the night when the last time I was in the saddle was on my tenth birthday."

He lifted one brow and his eyes swept over her. She sure had the attitude of a stubborn cowgirl. But the more he took her in, he noticed little things about her that made it clear she was as much of a city girl as the rest of them. "You don't belong out here," he mused. His statement wasn't meant to be offensive. In fact, it was more for his own thought process. This woman wasn't bred for country living. So why was her son working a ranch?

Before he had a chance to clarify his sentence, she scoffed. "I have just as much of a right to be here as you do. There is no rule or regulation that prevents anyone from moving out into the country." She let out a mirthless laugh. "You really are just as bad as they say you are. I bet you hate when outsiders move into your small little town and pollute the air with their city breath." She tapped her foot, her face growing more flushed during her tirade. "Let me tell you something, buddy. Everyone who lives here has been a transplant at one time or another and—"

Zeke held up his hand. "I'm going to have to stop you right there, ma'am. I meant no disrespect."

She snorted.

"What I meant was that you don't have a country bone in your body."

"So what?" she snapped. Her voice grew slightly shrill.

He dragged a hand through his hair and shook his head. "Never mind. Let's just get the ATV and head out. It's late, and no amount of explaining myself will fix this."

The woman made another disgruntled noise, but he'd already turned his back and was heading straight for where he kept the recreational vehicles and tractors.

He'd had a little bit of time before they arrived, and he'd been able to dig out some boxes of clothes he'd been planning on taking to the thrift store. They were probably musty as all get out, but this woman had lost everything. She couldn't turn up her nose at free clothing.

Then again, with her attitude, perhaps it wasn't too far out of the realm of possibility.

The only confirmation he got that she was following him was the shuffling footsteps behind him. He probably should have taken a look at her shoes to see if she needed something more practical. She'd definitely need something better than the pajamas she wore. Otherwise, she'd be going into town looking like she'd just left a slumber party.

Zeke stopped beside the ATV he had ready and waited for her. When she was close enough, he motioned for her to take the seat in the back. She gave him one dark look and then climbed onto the vehicle. As soon as he started the engine, they were off.

Ms. Birch sat back as far from him as humanly possible, and the only reason he knew this was because he couldn't feel her at all.

Not a whisper of her breath, not the warmth from her body, not her leg brushing against his. She couldn't possibly be comfortable in whatever contorted position she'd taken, but it wasn't for him to judge.

The drive to the cabin was uneventful, and by the time they'd arrived, the clouds were beginning to clear in the sky, revealing a portion of the moon. Zeke shut off the engine, then grabbed the box he'd strapped to the back and headed toward the door. The light was still on inside and he hadn't bothered to lock the door.

Zeke placed the box on the small kitchen table and immediately made his way to the bedroom. The bedding would need to be changed, and he had to gather some of his things along with a tent.

Grabbing onto the sheets, he yanked them hard, tossing them to the floor. Then he moved to the closet and pulled out a fresh set of bedding.

"What are you doing?"

He glanced up, finding Ms. Birch in the doorway. "I assume that's a rhetorical question."

She frowned at him, watching him as he moved to put a new fitted sheet on the bed. "No, I'm legitimately wondering what you're doing. It's the middle of the night."

"And these sheets need to be changed."

"You don't have to do that."

"Yes, I do," he said. There was no way he was going to allow a stranger to sleep in the bed that he'd been occupying.

She moved forward, heaving a sigh. "To make it clear, there was no need. It would have been just fine to change the bedding in the morning. Sleeping on dusty sheets isn't going to hurt me."

He slowed, his eyes jumping up to meet hers. "They're not dusty. They've been used recently."

Ms. Birch stopped after tugging one corner of the fitted sheet over the edge of the bed. "If someone is staying here, why would you offer for me to take it?"

"No one is staying here anymore."

The confusion in her gaze was almost what he would have called adorable. She was trying to make sense of it, but he wasn't about to clue her in. Someone like her wouldn't understand his need to escape the house on the hill.

Zeke completed making the bed and pulled the comforter over the top of the sheets. "I've got to get a few things and then I'll be out of your hair. There's a box of clothing on the kitchen table, and you'll find the fridge is stocked with anything you might immediately need. If you have any questions—"

"They can wait until morning, I assure you."

He nodded. "Right. Then just give me a few moments and I'll be out of here."

It didn't take long to gather the tent, bedroll, and various objects he'd need while setting up a campsite. It wouldn't be great putting everything together in the dark, but at least the storm had passed.

When he finally slipped out the door, Ms. Birch was nowhere in sight. She probably had found the bathroom. He couldn't blame her for wanting to clean up before getting off to bed. It had been one heck of a night, and they all deserved some much-needed rest.

ADELINE PLACED a cup and plate in front of Zeke, then hurried away only to return with a smaller plate with two slices of toast. "Did you hear about the old Mumford place? It was struck by lightning." She took a seat beside her husband and gave him a wide look. "It was so close. That could have been us."

Sean scooped up some eggs and took a bite, much to the disappointment of his son seated in the highchair at his side. The little tyke was coming up on eighteen months old, and it appeared he wanted any and all the food from his parents' plates these days. His small grubby hands reached for Sean's food, but Sean was now a seasoned father and he pushed the dish just out of reach before scooping a small serving of cereal onto the child's tray. "I think I saw when the lightning struck. We're lucky no one got hurt."

Adeline leaned forward in her seat. "So that's confirmed? No one was hurt?"

Sean nodded. "The chief filed a report early this morning, and Donahue told my mother. Apparently, the folks living there are new to the area."

She gasped. "That's so sad. I wasn't sure if anyone had bought the place yet."

"The young man who lived there with his mother works for us," Zeke muttered.

His daughter swung her gaze onto him. "What?"

"Tom Birch. Brielle hired him a few weeks ago."

Adeline covered her mouth with her hand. "That poor family. Where are they going to stay? Do they have family nearby?"

Zeke took a bite of his toast, savoring the buttery flavor before swallowing. "They're staying here."

It was like he'd just told everyone that the sky had turned neon pink overnight and that it was raining chickens for the way they were staring at him. If they'd had food in their mouth, he was certain he would have been required to perform the Heimlich maneuver.

"What?" Zeke questioned as he placed another piece of toast into his mouth.

"You're letting them stay here? Where? I didn't see anyone. Are they in one of the girls' rooms?"

He gave his daughter a disappointed look. Did she know nothing about him? "Tom is taking up with the men in the bunkhouse. Ms. Birch will be using the hunting cabin until further notice."

"The hunting cabin?" Adeline asked.

"There's a hunting cabin?" Sean said.

Adeline gave her husband a flat look before shifting her focus to her father. "I thought that place was all locked up. She can't possibly stay there until it gets aired out and cleaned."

"Well, according to her, it's better than sleeping in a partially burned-down home." Zeke settled deeper into his seat as he contemplated telling his daughter that the cleanliness of the cabin wasn't an issue. But the fact that she hadn't caught on to his sleeping there kept him quiet.

It wasn't her fault that she hadn't noticed. She'd been busy running a lot of the daily duties for the ranch and taking care of an energetic toddler. It was his other daughters—Brielle and Eloise—who would have been the ones to catch on first.

Zeke could have been miffed that his daughters didn't notice his absence, but he was more grateful that he'd been able to retreat from the craziness, the change, and the volume of noise that was now part of their everyday life around here. Though all but one of his daughters were married, they had a tendency to hover. They'd come for meals or spend the night. Their sense of family was such that they didn't seem quite ready to lose the kinship they'd developed with one another— something he ought to have been proud of.

There was just too much change happening far too fast. And his wife was supposed to be here for all of it.

His gaze landed on his grandson. Colt was a perfect blend of his mother and his father. Already Zeke could tell he would grow up to be stubborn, just like his parents, but he'd also have a good heart. Colt glanced toward him and froze. His toothy grin stretched across his face, and he slapped his hands down on the highchair tray three times.

Zeke smiled back, then turned to his food. "I'm going to be away from the ranch today. I've got a few things to do around the cabin." Namely, make sure there weren't any concerning animal tracks.

Adeline nodded. "I can come help clean it."

"No need. Based on what I noticed with Ms. Birch last night, she's going to have that whole place dusted and cleaned before I get out there." He wasn't quite certain that was something this woman would have done, but the last thing he needed was for his daughter to realize just how lived-in the place had been as of late. Not to mention the tent that was set up several meters away.

His daughter didn't argue, nor did she make any comments about him being absent more lately. That suited him just fine. He'd just come around for mealtime and save himself the discomfort the recent changes to his life had created.

4

Agatha

gatha wandered through the hunting cabin, her fingers trailing along the rustic furniture as she took in her surroundings. When she thought of a hunting cabin, she had only envisioned antlers displayed on the walls along with the occasional hunting rifle.

But this cabin was far more tasteful than she'd expected. It had a log cabin kind of feel with natural wood walls and ceiling. The light fixtures were modern with sterling silver hardware. Paintings of landscapes and regal deer hung on the wall.

Of course the couch and easy chair were upholstered in leather; that was a given. Surprisingly, the only sign that this cabin belonged to someone who liked to hunt was a family picture of a man with his young girls in the woods. They each held a small hunting rifle and wore brightly colored vests. The youngest appeared to be about four or five years old when the picture was taken.

Every single face smiled happily.

Agatha picked up the picture and stared at each of their small faces. She couldn't help the smile that touched her lips. It must have been difficult for Mr. Callahan to raise so many young women. She'd had a hard enough time being a single mother to one boy.

Quickly, she placed the picture back on the shelf and shook off the empathy she'd begun to feel for the man. He'd shown his true colors last night. He was bigoted and controlling. Just because he'd made some changes didn't mean he was the kind of person she would ever be friends with.

Her eyes lit on the box that he'd placed on the kitchen table. The early morning light seemed to put a spotlight on the cardboard through the slats of the blinds in the window. She stared at it, uncertain if she even wanted to open it. There was nowhere for her to go until her son came after his shift. He'd be able to take her to town to pick up a few things she might need while living here, which meant there was no point in her getting changed out of the pajamas she wore.

Except one thing.

She turned her nose to her shoulder, still smelling the smoke from the night before. That was one thing she knew she'd never be able to get rid of without washing her clothes. Thankfully, this small cabin had a modern laundry room. There was a stacked washer and dryer in what doubled as a broom closet. It had been a pleasant surprise when she'd discovered it this morning.

Exhaling, Agatha moved through the room toward the box. Whatever was in there likely wouldn't even fit. Her fingers wrapped around the edges of the cardboard and she pried the lid open. There was a stack of jeans on top, what looked like a few blouses beneath that, and some brightly colored clothing at the bottom. She glanced up toward the window, only seeing an expanse of nature.

The one thing she wanted to do today was head out to her

home and survey the damage in daylight hours. She would have several phone calls to make to her insurance provider and possible contractors.

Already she'd grown antsy just thinking about what she could be doing right now.

Then she had to contact Shane. He'd understand that her duties would have to be put on hold. There was no worry there. On top of it all, she really wanted to find another place to live. Somehow, knowing that Mr. Callahan was the one who put her here made her want to leave even more.

She turned back to the box and pulled out the top pair of jeans, finding they were a pair of overalls. They looked to be a bit big around the middle, but they were the right length. She could wear the T-shirt she'd slept in and just change out her pants. That would work out nicely.

Then she'd have to figure out a way to get to her home. If not that, she'd have to find her way to the ranch and catch a ride.

Muffled sounds from outside reached her ears and Agatha stiffened. She hugged the overalls to her chest and hurried to the wall where she could peek out the window to see who or what might be creeping outside.

At first, all she saw was an old-fashioned water pump. What she noticed next made her heart beat a little faster. Water droplets were falling from the pump to the ground as if it had been used recently.

Her eyes darted around the immediate area but found nothing besides bushes and trees. Someone was out there. Based on the ride they'd taken, she knew this cabin wasn't near anything else. Whoever was out there wasn't supposed to be.

Agatha made quick work of changing out of her pajama pants and into the overalls. She slipped her feet into the sandals she'd managed to grab on her way out of the burning house, then moved through the cabin to other windows in search of who was lurking.

Each time she stopped to check, she was both relieved and worried that she didn't see anyone.

Her phone was with her, but the battery was so low that she wasn't sure she'd be able to make a full phone call for help. Pressing her back against the wall, she searched the cabin for anything that might help her, and that was when her gaze landed on an old hunting rifle that leaned against the wall near the fireplace.

Making quick work, she slipped across the room and picked up the weapon. Whoever was out there didn't know she wasn't familiar with firearms. But they'd understand the tone of her voice, and they'd leave the moment she showed them she meant business.

Her hand trembled as she unlocked the door and poked her head outside. Inching along the small porch, she searched around the whole house, still finding no sign of anyone or anything. Had it all been in her imagination?

Just as she was about to lower the weapon, the sound of what could only be the snapping of a twig drew her attention.

She held her breath and swung the rifle around to point it in the direction of that sound, only to come face-to-face with none other than Zeke Callahan.

Her heart thrummed, pumping faster and harder than it probably had in her entire life. Her palms were clammy, but she held the weapon steady. Eyes narrowing, she stared at him with accusation. "What are you doing here?"

Mr. Callahan didn't seem fazed at all. He hadn't even raised his hands in the air to show he didn't intend harm.

What was wrong with him?

"You gonna lower that weapon so I can get back to work?" His voice was calm and collected, smooth. His eyes locked onto hers, and she found herself complying with what he'd requested. "Thank you." He nodded toward the gun. "Did you even check to see if that thing was loaded?"

She stared down at the rifle and her cheeks heated. "I didn't think I had to."

He lifted a brow, holding out his hand. "There are safety precautions when using a firearm. You know that, right?"

Agatha shoved the gun at him. "Of course I do."

"Have you ever handled a hunting rifle before?"

She glanced at the weapon once more. "Well, not one like that."

He lifted a brow. She didn't know how he knew, but he did. She'd never seen the need to operate a firearm before. Well, before she moved to the country. There were moments when she wondered if perhaps she should take a class so she could fend off coyotes that she'd heard could make their way out of the mountains.

"Fine," she conceded. "I've never shot a gun before."

He lifted the rifle. "This one might seem old, but it's still very much in working order. The ammunition goes in here, and..." He pulled back on part of the gun and tilted it toward her. "As you can see, this one is loaded. You were one trigger pull away from putting a hole right through me."

Agatha's stomach dropped. "Who in their right mind leaves a loaded weapon lying around?"

Mr. Callahan tilted his head, a ghost of a smile touching his lips. "You're staying in a hunting cabin. As such, there will be various hunting tools at your disposal."

"Don't you have a safe or something you can put it in?" She was deflecting and she knew it. This wasn't her home. This was his. And she had no right to tell him how to care for it.

He moved the rifle from one hand to the other and nodded. "Of course. I'll lock it up if that makes you feel more comfortable."

"Thank you." She crossed her arms, and her thoughts

immediately shifted to why she was holding the weapon in the first place. "Were you the one who was lurking around the cabin?" Her voice dripped with accusation. "Are you *spying* on me?"

She didn't know what she expected, but it wasn't his laughter. Agatha stiffened, her eyes narrowing into slits. "Just because you let me stay here doesn't mean you get to spy on me like that."

He shook his head. "I've done nothing of the sort. I came out here to check on the property. There have been some reports of wolves and coyotes wandering the outskirts of the woods around here."

Agatha's gaze shifted to her surroundings. "Do you think I'll be safe out here?"

"As long as you don't take unnecessary walks out into the woods past dark, you should be just fine."

"Well, it shouldn't matter in a few days. I'm going to check with my boss and that motel to see if there are any other options for me." When she brought her eyes back to Mr. Callahan, she was surprised to find his expression had darkened. She couldn't possibly have offended him. That was silly.

Right?

"Is there something wrong?"

He worked his jaw, then brushed past her as he muttered, "Nope."

She followed him inside. "Yes, there is. Don't lie to me. I can tell when there's something going on and you're holding it back."

"If you're so sure, then why even ask?" He made his way into the house and headed straight for a door that she'd not explored yet. It opened up to a small bedroom. There was a twin bed, but that was where the description of a bedroom stopped. There was a worktable with stacked boxes of ammunition and gunsmithing tools. More hunting pictures hung on the walls and were displayed on the side table of the bed. There was even a display of antlers hanging over the head of the bed.

Mr. Callahan headed directly to a tall black safe and twisted a knob until something clicked. He pulled open the safe to reveal several more menacing-looking rifles, along with a few small ones. The smaller ones were in a variety of colors—pink, purple, and girly camo.

He placed the gun inside, then shut the safe and turned the dial. "There," he muttered, "you're safe."

Her eyes lingered on the safe and she started to wonder if she shouldn't have said anything. If there were coyotes and wolves wandering the premises, then she would be safer with a means to protect herself.

"If there's nothing else you need, then I'll be heading on my way."

She glanced at him again, then shook her head. "That's it."

"Fine," he grunted, then moved toward the doorway. Mr. Callahan disappeared into the hallway before she came to her senses.

"Actually, I do have something I need." She chased after him, catching him before he exited the cabin altogether. He stood in the doorway, expectant. She pulled herself up sharply, keeping a reasonable distance between them. "I wanted to go to my place... see the damage."

He shook his head. "That's not a good idea."

Her defenses immediately went up and she placed her hands on her hips. "Why not? It's my home, and I need to take stock of what happened."

"I'm not saying you can't go. I'm saying that you shouldn't go yet."

"That's ridiculous. I can't get my insurance to do anything until I know what to claim."

Mr. Callahan stared at her for what felt like an eternity, then shook his head again. "That's what the fire report will do. You are better off letting them sort this out before you head over."

She snorted. "If you think I'm the kind of woman who will sit by, twiddling her thumbs instead of rolling up her sleeves and doing what it takes to get things done, then you have no idea who you're dealing with."

"Clearly."

His single statement brought her up short. "Pardon?"

He dragged his hand down his face and let out a sigh. "Let me guess, you're going over there whether I like it or not."

"You bet I am. You have zero control over what I do."

"And what if I told you that you'd be making a target out of yourself?"

She scoffed. "A target for *what*? The animals?"

He merely looked at her like the answer to her question was obvious.

"Then give me one of your guns and I'll protect myself. I haven't seen any animals out this way so far. I'm sure I'll be fine."

A sigh burst from his lips once more. "You're not going to listen to reason, are you?"

"Mr. Callahan, I am more than capable of taking care of myself. I have dealt with the wolves of the city. I think I can handle a few furry animals out here. You can either help me get there or take me to your ranch so I can catch a ride. Either way, I'm going home."

They glared at each other, the battle of wills raging between them. For a moment she thought he wouldn't back down and she'd have to actually tromp through the woods in her sandals and overalls until she found the edge of her property.

But then he conceded. "I'll take you on the ATV after I finish making the rounds. The least you could do is give me that."

"Fine."

His eyes dipped to her feet as if he'd heard her thoughts earlier. "You're gonna want some more sensible shoes."

"Too bad. I'm assuming they've all burned up with the rest of my belongings."

"Check the closet in that spare room. There might be some boots you can borrow." He moved to leave, but she stopped him.

"Can I use your phone? I have a few calls I want to make."

Zeke pulled his phone from his pocket. "The passcode is four six one nine." With that, he pulled the door shut and headed around the side of the house.

Agatha expelled a heavy breath and shook out her free hand. She hadn't realized just how taxing it would be to go up against the infamous Zeke Callahan.

Well, at least she'd come out on top.

5

____

Zeke

She's just some woman who doesn't know any better.

An irritating, hard-headed, beautiful woman who could pull off a pair of overalls like nobody's business.

Zeke groaned, rubbing the back of his neck as he stomped through the overgrowth surrounding the hunting cabin. Thankfully, there were no new tracks he needed to be concerned about, but that didn't mean he wasn't going to be vigilant. It didn't matter what Agatha said. She couldn't go up against a pack of wolves on her best day.

He slowed his steps, forcing himself to focus more on the task at hand than on the woman who clearly couldn't bother to be appreciative of what he'd given her. What kind of person refuses free lodging in a place like this? His fingers trailed through the leaves of a nearby bush. In just a few more months, the green would burst into bright red coloring. The shrubs weren't native out here. They'd been planted by Evelyn when he'd dragged her to the hunting cabin occasionally. Besides his daughters, they were the last remaining memory he had of her —one more reason he preferred to be out here when things got tough under his own roof.

Evelyn would have made sure that Agatha was taken care of. That was just her nature. And if Agatha had insisted on leaving, she would have found a reason to make her stay. Well, he wasn't his late wife. Zeke didn't have the magic touch, and if Agatha wanted to leave, then who was he to tell her no?

His scowl returned as he gathered some fallen twigs. The woman needed a refresher course in manners, but he wasn't going to be the one to do it. The sooner she took off, the sooner he'd have the hunting cabin to himself. At least he could have that.

With arms full of branches, he trudged back to the cabin. It was quiet. Not even the animals chattered in the trees. His heart immediately thrummed to life, and he nearly dropped the wood he'd gathered to go in search of the woman he felt responsible for—until he heard her voice.

"What do you mean you're booked out for the next six weeks? The rodeo doesn't start for two."

Zeke came up short, pressing his back against the wood siding and straining his ears to hear her side of the conversation.

"But you *do* have openings for the next two weeks. What if I take one of those rooms and you let me know if there's a cancelation."

He shook his head with disgust. This place was like a private getaway. What would push her to upend her life more than it had already been? Even if she took a room now, she'd be booted when the rodeo came to town and then what? She'd have to find somewhere else to live.

Well, he wasn't about to put a hold on his life while she bounced from place to place. He'd put his foot down. She either stayed or she left. There was no in-between.

"That's ridiculous. I've never heard of a place *not* having cancelations. You must have a few rooms you use as backup."

Zeke snorted. This woman didn't know just how small Copper Creek was. She might as well head the few hours to the city and stay there.

Agatha hung up and let out a growl.

Pushing against the building, Zeke did his best to school his features. The last thing this little firecracker would want to see was the glee he had from knowing he had been right. He dropped the kindling on the wood pile, causing her to gasp as she spun to face him.

Her face was flushed and her eyes flashed with fury, though it didn't appear to be directed at him. Dusting off his hands, he nodded to the phone. "You make all the calls you need to? Insurance? A contractor?"

He knew she'd probably figured he'd overheard her last conversation, a point that was made clearer by the way the coloring in her face deepened. She gritted her teeth as she glanced in the direction where her home would be. "Actually, I was calling the different hotels, motels, and B&Bs in the area." She didn't bother to look in his direction then. She probably knew that he wouldn't be pleased with that information.

Zeke grunted, turning his back to her as he adjusted the wood pile. "It might have been smarter to call the insurance company first. I could have told you the rodeo was going to have all the spare rooms around here."

"Yeah, well, you didn't," she muttered.

"I've just about had enough of this talk." He whirled around, his hard eyes taking in every inch of her. "I've offered you nothing but charity, and you're choosing to spit in my face. What is so wrong with me that you can't stand to stay even a few weeks on my property?"

Her eyes fluttered wide, then she looked away. "It's not about that."

"Isn't it? You have a place to live. Granted, it's not what you might be used to, but it's good enough when what you have is *nothing*."

"You're right," she spat back. "I *have* nothing. No clothes. No furniture. Not even a bed to call my own. But that's not the worst part. All I have are the memories."

"What memories? You haven't been living in Copper Creek that long. You couldn't have made too many memories in that house."

Her face flushed even more than he thought possible. "I didn't grow up in the digital age, Mr. Callahan. Everything from my past was in that home. And now it's... gone."

That brought him up short. She was talking about pictures. Mementos.

Zeke let a whispered curse slip between his lips. She was dealing with a lot more than he'd originally considered. And now he felt like the bad guy. He'd been pushing her to do something when she was already teetering at the brink of not being able to handle any of this.

When he glanced up at her, she swiped at her face with the back of her hand. He hadn't caught any tears. As far as he knew, she hadn't even shed one since the fire. But he wouldn't have been surprised if that was what she'd been doing when he glanced over at her.

He was torn.

Torn between the instinct to pull her into his arms and tell her everything would be okay and keeping his distance because he was probably the last person she wanted to see right about now.

Zeke averted his eyes, returning to the gruff man as was his reputation. "You ready? We can check out your place and see what's left of it. You can use my phone for pictures to send to your insurance adjuster."

Agatha nodded, her composure regained. Neither one of

them spoke on the ride, probably because there was nothing to be said. She was dealing with a loss that he didn't understand. Losing his wife meant losing his partner in this world. But he still had those memories—the home videos and the photo albums.

Thinking of losing any of that put a weight in the pit of his stomach. In order to ease that discomfort, he focused instead on the foliage. Between this property and the next, he could take note of the trees, bushes, wildflowers, and anything else that bothered to sprout up along the trail. If Agatha hadn't lost her whole world, she might have enjoyed this scenic trip. He found himself racking his brain for anything he might be able to do to make her feel better.

And he couldn't figure out why that was.

Agatha was a stranger. They didn't know each other well enough for him to do something like that for her. What was she to him but just a neighbor?

Her hands tightened around his middle when they went over a bump, and even over the engine, he heard a quick intake of breath. Zeke fought a smile. He shouldn't be enjoying this ride. The poor woman had lost everything and could barely stand him. He needed to get his head on straight.

Just as they came over the ridge of a hill, the charred remains of the back side of the house rose into view.

Another gasp ripped from Agatha's lips just behind his ear. Her body tensed, clinging to him as if he were the only thing that stood between her and the heartache she was experiencing. When he pulled the vehicle to a stop, she clambered off and strode toward the building as if pushed by a force that was not her own—straight for the back entrance.

Zeke shut off the engine and charged after her. He grasped onto her wrist and pulled her to a sudden stop. "What in tarnation do you think you're doing?"

She stared at him, not quite seeing him. Then clarity

flooded her gaze and she threw her finger toward the building. "I'm going in there to see if there's anything I can salvage."

He shook his head. "There's nothing you can do. Even if something wasn't burned, it's bound to be damaged by the smoke or the water. That place was lit up like the Fourth of July."

"I don't care," she stammered, her eyes shifting to the building. "If there's anything in there—"

"It's not safe." His voice was harder than he anticipated, evidenced by the way she stared at him like he'd nearly bitten her head off.

"You can't tell me what to do on my own property," she snapped back, yanking her arm away from him. "If I want to go inside, I'm going to do it."

He blocked her path, glowering at her. "I told you I'd bring you up here, but I won't allow you to go and get yourself hurt. I'm not going to be held liable for you choosing feelings over smarts."

Her mouth fell open, then quickly shifted into disdain. "Fine. You can leave and it won't be your fault. My property. My body. My problem."

He let out a growl. "Stay here." Zeke spun around, marching toward the back door.

"Where do you think you're going?"

He stopped, faced her, then tossed his phone at her. "Insurance. Contractor."

Agatha caught the device, and he hurried up the steps into her house.

The walls were blackened from the ceiling down. Zeke pulled his shirt collar up to his nose, but it didn't ward off the heavy scent of smoke in the air. The kitchen was in terrible shape. Cabinets hung open, charred and lopsided where the fire had ripped through them. Broken dishes lay on the floor. A plastic container was half melted onto the countertop. Overhead there was one gaping hole in the ceiling up to the second floor but no way to tell what room it was.

He stepped over shattered glass, careful not to disturb too much. He made it to the stairs, but they were in worse shape than he'd thought. If he even tried to climb them, he'd fall through. Instead, he continued on the main floor until he reached the front of the house. Besides the evidence of smoke damage, the room appeared normal.

A couch, a loveseat, and a few chairs surrounded a coffee table. On the couch a throw blanket had been tossed in such a way it had probably been laid there by a designer. Zeke rolled his eyes. Agatha was probably the kind of person who liked to stage things to look haphazard.

His boot snagged on the throw, dragging it from the couch and onto the floor when he wandered past. A large leather-bound book had been hidden beneath it. That was the kind of book that contained the exact thing Agatha had been so heart-broken over losing.

Zeke backtracked and stared at the book, then up at the door he'd come through. If this was what he thought it was, then he might have just found something that could jumpstart her healing process.

Slowly reaching for the book as if at any moment it might take the form of a snake and launch at him, he inched closer. His fingers wrapped around it, and he pulled the bulky object into his hands. With a flick of his wrist, he flipped it open, finding exactly what he thought it would contain.

The photos in the front were older, much older than Agatha could have been. They were yellowed and faded, showing stern faces of people who could only be her relatives. Zeke snapped the book shut and strode toward the front entrance, opting not to traipse through the rubble in the kitchen. He headed out onto the porch, stopping suddenly as he came across Agatha pacing while on the phone once again.

"Nine months? How on earth can you be nine months out?" Her eyes darted toward Zeke and away so quickly she definitely hadn't seen the book he carried. "I *have* called other contractors. You're telling me you can't start on a rebuild for nearly a year. What do you—" She stopped herself, smoothing her voice until it sounded like a shell of what it was. "Thank you for your time. Yes, I understand."

Agatha got off the phone and let out a ferocious growl that would have put a cougar to shame.

Maybe she really could handle herself with the wolves and coyotes.

Her eyes landed on him and she let out an exasperated breath. "No one can help me rebuild. There are no other places where I can live. The only people who are cooperating with me were the ones I thought I might have to fight."

"The insurance folks?"

She nodded. "I can't believe this is happening. One lightning storm and..." Her voice broke. "I don't know what I'm going to do." Her gaze flitted to meet his, then dropped to the contents of his hands. "What's that?"

Each step he took made the wood creak beneath his feet until he found himself on solid ground. He held out the photo album. "It smells like a campfire, but it was covered by a blanket."

Agatha snatched the album from his hands, eyes wide and brimming with tears. "Where did you find this?" she demanded in a hushed whisper.

"In the living room."

Tears tumbled from her eyes down her cheeks, and she shook her head. "That's not possible. It was in a box upstairs in the spare room where the lightning hit." Her fingertips traced the leather cover as her bright eyes lifted to meet his.

"Dunno what to tell you. I found it in the living room under a blanket."

Without warning, she threw herself at him, the book wedged between them.

His hands shot out to his sides initially, unsure of what he should do.

But then her body started shaking, racked with sobs.

Sobs of relief? Sorrow? Joy?

He couldn't tell. Carefully, he wrapped his arms around Agatha and held her, letting her expel every last ounce of ache she'd been holding onto since this whole ordeal began.

She could take as long as she needed. He wasn't going anywhere.

6

———

Agatha

*I*t wasn't hard to lose all track of time.

Agatha could have clung to Zeke for an hour, three hours, an entire day, and she wouldn't have realized it. There was a part of her that was perfectly content to be wrapped in his strong arms and allow herself this moment of weakness.

Then that moment passed.

What was she doing?

This was Zeke Callahan—the rough around the edges man who everyone in town had a thing or two to say regarding his temperament.

Cautiously, she extricated herself from his embrace. Without meeting his gaze, she mumbled, "Thank you for finding the book."

He made a noise that didn't sound like much more than what an animal might make.

Quickly wiping at her eyes, she glanced at him, then down

to the album in her hands. "You don't know what this means to me."

"I'm sure I could wager a guess."

She let out a soft laugh. "Yeah, I suppose so."

Zeke peered up at the house, his eyes narrowing slightly. "The stairs are unusable. I'm assuming if you have anything upstairs, it's taken the brunt of the smoke damage. Where is your bedroom?"

"Upstairs," she murmured.

"Right. So that means all your clothing and bedding won't be usable."

"Not likely," she sighed. This was what she'd figured when they'd arrived. The fire started upstairs in the back of the house and swept through the house a heck of a lot faster than she would have thought. "I guess I'm going to have to—"

"You're going shopping."

She stilled. "What?" The single word escaped her lips with a small laugh riding its tail.

"I needed to head to town anyway. I can take you."

Agatha shook her head. "I can't. I don't have any way to pay for it. Everything I owned, including my wallet, was in my room. It'll be a few days before I can get replacements. And my bank isn't based in Copper Creek. I hadn't started moving things over to a local credit union yet." She flushed at that confession. What person moves out to a place like this and doesn't make that change right away?

"My treat." Zeke threw the statement at her before brushing past her and heading around back where they'd parked.

Marching after him, she stumbled in the oversized boots and nearly collided with him in her haste. "What? No. I'm not going to let you do that."

Zeke stopped and faced her, his expression curious. "Why not?"

She stiffened. "You're asking me why I won't let you spend money on me?"

"Yeah. Let's go with that. Why can't I give you some money for new clothes?"

"Well," she sputtered, "for one thing you're not my husband."

"So?"

The heat that came along with those words was excruciating, and it took every ounce of power she had to maintain eye contact with him. "You don't owe me anything. I'm fine. I lost my house and my belongings, but that's what insurance is for. I'll get everything sent to me, and in the meantime, I'll wear this." Agatha gestured toward her outfit with mild contempt.

"Are you Christian?"

Her head snapped up at his forward question. "What?"

"I'm beginning to think you need your ears checked. Are. You. Christian?"

"What does that have anything to do with anything?" she demanded. "It's none of your business if I'm Christian or not."

"Just answer the question."

She crossed her arms, a scowl creeping across her features. "I was raised Christian, yes."

"Then is it not true that we should accept service as much as we give it?"

Agatha gaped at him, hating the way he could make a smug smile look almost attractive. He'd caught her, and he knew it. There were no other arguments she could make to his statement.

"And as someone who has lost so much, would it not be pertinent for you to humble yourself and accept help from a friend?"

"We're not—"

"On top of that, wouldn't dismissing my offer be just as

detrimental? You would then be taking away the opportunity I have to provide some service as well."

She snapped her mouth shut, gritting her teeth so hard her jaw ached. Once again, he made a point she profusely agreed with. If their situations had been swapped, she'd demand something similar.

He crossed his arms, and his smile widened. "I have more than enough to provide for my family and friends. I help out in the community where I can. And if a damsel in distress needs some extra help, I will offer it."

"I'm not some damsel in—"

"Besides," Zeke continued, "it's only money. I doubt you could spend more than some of my daughters when they go on a shopping spree." He jerked his head over toward the ATV. "Come on. Let's get back to my place and we can take the truck. Somehow, I don't think you'd want to ride to town with your arms around me." He paused, giving her another funny look. "Unless you're into that."

She made a disgruntled sound, charging past him. He'd won this time. She couldn't argue with his logic in this instance, but that wouldn't stop her from putting up a fight any chance she got.

AGATHA KEPT her eyes trained out her window as Zeke pulled the truck to a stop. She'd managed to avoid any probing questions and small talk the entire ride to town. She still wasn't thrilled about accepting his help and decided long before she got into his truck that she'd figure out a way to pay him back for his generosity. There was just one thing she needed to make clear before they exited the vehicle.

Facing him, she forced her voice to remain steady. "I'm

under no assumption that you aren't well aware of my situation."

He was flipping through the cash in his wallet as she spoke, which both infuriated her and gave her a small amount of relief. He wasn't looking at her so she could speak her mind without feeling unnerved beneath his stare.

"There are no vacancies within fifty miles of this place. The rodeo is coming, and I need a place to stay." She briefly closed her eyes, recalling the conversation they'd had earlier when she'd insisted on making her stay as short as possible. Boy, was she eating her words right about now. "And the contractors are going to be out almost a year. I think I might be able to stay somewhere else when the rodeo leaves, but until then..." She waited for him to look in her direction.

When she didn't speak, he finally lifted his eyes. They were the eyes of someone who had seen a lot in his life. He'd gone through so much, and she only knew tiny pieces of it. A flutter erupted in her chest, recalling the way he'd held her—how he'd found the most precious item in her home.

Agatha needed to push through. "I'd like to stay at your hunting cabin as long as you will allow."

His brows pulled together. "I'm sorry? What made you think that anything had changed?"

She blinked rapidly. "I beg your pardon?" Then she grimaced, realizing just how often she had been asking him to repeat himself.

Zeke reached for her hand, pulling it toward him, palm up. He placed some bills there, then folded her fingers over. "You're welcome to stay at that cabin as long as you see fit. There were no conditions. Now, go on and get some new clothes. I'm headed to the hardware store across the street. If you get done before me, we can meet up here, or over there. Your choice." He grabbed his cowboy hat from the seat between them and placed it on his head. "Go on, then."

The hesitation lasted only momentarily before she launched herself from his truck and hurried around the front. Zeke exited as well, then nodded to her before he headed across the street. Agatha glanced down at the cash in her hand, expecting to see twenties. A gasp tore from her throat, finding a wad of hundreds.

Her head snapped up, but her voice died in her throat as he disappeared into the shop. There was no way she could spend all of this on clothing. Not in one trip, anyway. But there would be no demanding he take it back. She had the strongest feeling he'd shove the money down her throat if he could. Perhaps Zeke wasn't as bad as everyone had made him out to be—a little rough around the edges, but a good man, nevertheless.

She didn't realize a smile had crossed her face until she entered the small clothing shop and the harried chatter dropped to nothing. The room went cold. Agatha glanced toward the storefront where the chirping had been taking place, only to find two women. One stood behind the counter and the other in front, leaning over it with her elbows resting in the middle.

Now, they both stared at her. The one in front of the counter stood slowly, a smile stretching across her face. "Welcome to Courtney's. Let us know if there's anything we can help you with, hun."

Agatha nodded, offering a faint smile. When she turned to peruse the aisles of clothing, the whispering started up again. She didn't catch much, but the words that she could make out were such that it was clear she was the topic of their conversation.

Words like "Zeke, new woman, dating, fire" were tossed around as if her right to privacy didn't exist in these four walls. Clearly, this town was far too small for something like a house-fire to remain a secret—especially when Zeke Callahan let the poor woman living there stay on his property.

By the time Agatha had gathered all the items she wanted, she was fuming. Had billows of steam been rising off her shoulders and her head, she wouldn't have been surprised in the slightest.

The women stopped their gossip. Apparently, they had no clue just how bad even a whisper could carry in this small shop. The one who'd welcomed her smiled as she took the clothes draped over her arm. "Did you find everything you were looking for?" The woman's eyes darted out the front window toward the hardware store where Zeke was. It was almost too obvious what she meant by that backhanded comment.

Agatha wasn't going to play their game.

Or maybe she would. She just wouldn't play by their rules.

"Actually, yes, thank you. It's amazing what you can find when you're not even looking for it." There. Let them take that statement and run with it. The gossipers should beware. If they wanted to play with fire, they shouldn't mess with her. She'd already been burned.

The women glanced at one another with surprise and perhaps a little greed. They had most definitely taken the bait.

Armed with her change and the bags of clothing, Agatha headed across the street toward the store where Zeke would be found. Hopefully, he wouldn't mind the games she'd set in motion. Though she couldn't see him being the type who would care about the local gossip. Maybe he'd even be amused that she beat them at their own game.

Her steps were lighter as she shouldered into the hardware store and immediately turned down the nearest aisle. Zeke wasn't readily visible, and she didn't hear his gruff voice. Agatha stood on her toes, glancing up and down the aisles but then stopped when something bright yellow caught her eye.

Surrounded by several different variations was a little yellow birdhouse. It had a blue roof and a little red-painted post for the birds to perch on before they entered. This birdhouse had to be the cutest thing she'd seen in a long time. It was bright and sunny, and it was exactly what she needed in her life.

Agatha grabbed the house from the hook where it hung and continued wandering through the store. By the time she made it through the whole place, she finally found Zeke at the front, speaking with another older gentleman. He leaned against the counter, speaking with the man in hushed tones.

Her movement caught the attention of the shop owner and his focus shifted to her, which drew Zeke's attention as well. He glanced over his shoulder, and for a moment she thought he might smile. Instead, he straightened, said one more thing to the man and dropped his palm to the counter.

Agatha approached slower this time. "I hope I'm not interrupting."

"No, you're fine." Zeke motioned to the birdhouse. "You getting that?"

She lifted it and a smile filled her face. "Yes."

Zeke exchanged a glance with the man, but they said nothing. What a strange reaction to her getting a birdhouse. The whole ride back to the ranch, she burned with the questions of why he might react to her that way. On top of that, why was he at the hardware store, but he didn't purchase anything? He hadn't been at the front of the shop when she'd gotten there either.

When they turned onto the road that would lead them to the ranch house, she nearly asked him what all of it meant, but then she stopped herself. None of it was her business. Yes, they were a little closer now—mostly due to her losing her cool earlier. But they weren't close enough for her to confront him on any of it.

The truck came to a stop, and she held onto her birdhouse tighter. "Sorry."

"What are you sorry for?"

She bit back a smile. "I might have turned you into a spectacle."

Zeke froze mid-grasp of the door handle. "Care to elaborate?"

Biting her lip, Agatha's eyes cut to meet his. "I might have said a few things to the ladies at that clothing store today."

His eyes narrowed, and she flushed.

"In my defense, they were clearly gossiping about you and me already. I just said a few things that would keep them busy for a little while." She let out a nervous laugh, waiting for him to get angry or tell her she had overstepped.

Instead, he let out a sigh. "Courtney and her daughter Chloe are terrible gossips. Whatever you said, they probably deserved it." He pushed open the door and climbed out, leaving her to revel in his approval, if she could call it that. Zeke had more in common with her than she thought.

7

———

Zeke

Zeke paused outside of the truck and took a deep breath before releasing it. If only doing so would quell the nerves that had gone rogue. This woman was proving to be more problematic than he'd anticipated.

It wasn't just his instinct to take care of her due to her current predicament. There was something else brewing whenever he was around her. He went from viewing her as a nuisance to someone he might actually like.

What was happening to him?

Before Agatha had been thrown into his life, he had been content. Yes, he was avoiding his daughters and their spouses or soon-to-be spouses, but he'd been just fine.

Now, his heart was in an uproar whenever he saw the slightest hint of sadness on this woman's face. His chest tightened whenever she looked at him like he was someone who could mean something to her. And he felt lighter than ever when she did or said something that made him want to laugh out loud.

Courtney wouldn't let any amount of gossip stay locked away for long. Guaranteed, whatever Agatha had said to her was going to get out before supper. Already, he couldn't wait until the time when he sat around the table with his daughters and they brought it up.

He turned just as Agatha climbed out of the truck. She motioned to the bags in the back with uncertainty. "Are we taking the ATV back to the cabin? Or is there a road we can take your truck on?

"There's a road."

She hovered, that confounded birdhouse still in her hands. He could see the cogs turning in her head. She wanted to know something. With his luck it would have nothing to do with the road or the truck but be something else entirely.

His expression tightened, and he nodded toward the barn. "I've got a few things to check on. If you'd like to tag along, I'll show you around." Not waiting for a response, Zeke moved past her. If she wanted to come, she would. That's what a normal person would do. Otherwise, she'd stay back and wait.

Then again, Agatha Birch wasn't normal. Maybe he shouldn't have given her a choice.

He got about a dozen steps away when he heard her quick steps behind him. Good. She'd gone with the smart move. If she'd opted to stay back, there was no telling what kind of trouble she might find herself in.

Agatha fell in step beside him, still holding the birdhouse. He eyed it, not understanding why it seemed to bother him so much. It was just a few pieces of wood that had been glued and nailed together and then painted.

You know better than that. The birdhouse reminds you of her.
Evelyn.

Zeke pushed away the thought of his late wife and the fact

that Agatha reminded him so much of her. They were not the same person, and they never would be. His Evelyn was long gone. She wasn't coming back.

"Do you not like birds?"

Zeke glanced at her out of the corner of his eye. "Why do you ask that?" Here it was. She wanted to know more about him and this was the path she'd taken. One slip, and he'd go down the rabbit hole that was his life.

Agatha lifted the birdhouse she carried and smiled as she stared at it. Her fingers traced the edges thoughtfully. "Because you didn't seem thrilled I got this."

He shot a look toward the glorified craft box and grunted. "I don't care one way or another."

"You're lying."

The tightness in his chest worsened as if she'd managed to find some invisible entity that could wrap its claws around the organs housed there and make it near impossible for him to breathe. His walls came up, and he stopped to face her. "Who are you to make such an assumption? You don't know me any better than you would a man off the street."

"Maybe," she shot back, "or maybe I've been watching you, and every time you look at the birdhouse, you look like you're about ready to pass out."

He stared at her blankly. Was he so transparent? He didn't think so, but then again, he wasn't on the outside looking in. And he didn't have the abilities most women did. "Okay. I'll play. Why do you think I hate birds?"

"Like I said. You can't look at this thing without appearing sick to your stomach. So either you hate birds, or this birdhouse makes you feel uncomfortable."

He crossed his arms as he came to a stop directly in front of the barn. His eyes narrowed, but in that moment he knew better than to believe that he was going to get out of this scot-free. "I was telling the truth when I told you I don't care one way or another about that silly thing. Bird houses aren't natural, so I guess I don't have a particular fondness about them being placed on my property, but in the end I really couldn't care less."

Agatha snorted. "See? Right there. Another lie. You don't want them on your property, but at the same time, you don't care? That's a conflict if I ever heard one."

He sighed, removing the hat from his head before he ran a hand over his mussed hair. "I don't care if you have a birdhouse. There. That's your answer."

"But it isn't—"

With each passing second, he felt like he was being backed into a corner. She was pushing him there, blocking his exits and making him realize he really didn't have much control anymore.

At least that was how it felt inside his chest where his heart was frantically trying to gain some ground.

Zeke slapped his hat onto his head and glowered at her. "If you really must know, my wife was just like you." He waved his hand with a flick of his wrist in the general direction of the birdhouse. "That's exactly the sort of thing she would have bought on a whim. In fact, I'm sure we have half a dozen of them lying around the property somewhere. So you just wasted your money."

He expected her to get defensive and upset over his statement.

Or at least she'd be embarrassed.

Zeke steeled himself for that exact thing to happen, all the while bringing up his own defenses. He didn't talk about his late wife with anyone except his daughters, and even that was limited. It was all part of how he moved on, and it had worked out just fine. His eyes narrowed as he waited for Agatha to jump at his throat to tell him he needed to lighten up.

But none of that happened. She smirked at him, shaking

her head. "Actually, I wasted *your* money." Then with a flourish, she pulled a few bills from her back pocket. "I don't know why you felt the need to give me so much. I wasn't buying a whole new wardrobe."

"That's exactly what that money was for." He pushed the money she held out toward him back. "You lost everything in that fire. You needed to make sure you could replace the whole thing."

This time she threw her head back and the laughter that spilled from her throat was such that he didn't know how to respond. She was clearly laughing at him for some reason. He wasn't sure what it was about, but he didn't like it.

If there was one thing he hated, it was being made a fool of. And here he stood in front of her, unsure of what was so terribly funny that she had to react with such flippant disregard.

Agatha brought her eyes back to meet his, her soft snickers still throwing him off guard. "There is zero chance I'm going to be able to replace my whole wardrobe with one stop at that boutique clothing shop. They *definitely* didn't carry everything I needed. And I wasn't going to spend all that money either. You gave me way too much."

He opened his mouth to protest, ready to put her in her place like he had last time, but she cut him off.

"I really appreciate what you've done for me so far, but I can't keep on accepting this charity without doing something for you in return. I don't know. Maybe you could help me figure out something. I work in Public Relations now, but I grew up in the country. I'm sure you could put me to work—"

"Over my dead body." This ridiculousness had gone on long enough. He was the one helping her right now. She'd lost so much, and yet here she was, expecting him to force her to work off what he had offered? Absolutely not.

She snapped her mouth shut and stared at him with wide

eyes. Again, he'd used a tone sharper than intended and clearly, that was something she didn't appreciate. Well, he didn't care.

"You are here as my guest. I'm not going to have you do anything. All that you have been given has been from the goodness of my heart, and I'll not have you brushing that aside like it means nothing."

"I wasn't brushing it aside—"

"Then why don't we finish this tour and get you back to the cabin, shall we?" He ducked into the barn, making note in his head of the chores that had been completed and that which still needed to be done. The animals had been fed. Most of the stalls had been cleaned. There were a few horses out getting their exercise. Everything was on track and working like a well-oiled machine.

"This place is bigger than I thought," Agatha said.

Out of the corner of his eye, he noticed her fall into step beside him. "The size isn't what matters. It's the team I have running it." He stopped and motioned to the barn. "None of this would be possible without my family and the men I've come to know like family. Granted, some of the newer hires are still strangers to me, but in time I'm sure they will become the same." He wasn't certain, but he thought he saw a ghost of a smile touch her lips.

She shifted her weight from one foot to the other, her head tilting as she stared up at him. "You're not what I expected, Mr. Callahan."

"What is that supposed to mean?"

She opened her mouth, but they were interrupted.

"Mom? What are you doing here? Is everything okay?"

They both turned to find her son heading toward them, leading a horse by a rope. He guided the animal into a stall and hurried forward, his concerned gaze darting from his mother to Zeke. "What happened?"

"Nothing happened, dear." Agatha gestured toward Zeke

with a smile. "Mr. Callahan took me to town so I could get a few things, and then we were going to head back to the hunting cabin so I could get settled in."

A flurry of emotions crossed Thomas's face. The one Zeke noted most was distrust. Then again, Zeke didn't know Thomas as well as his other wranglers. He might just be concerned for his mother. "I could have taken you after my shift. I needed to go to town, too."

"Oh, nonsense, Thomas. You're busy enough as it is. You don't need to worry about me."

"Yes, I do." He moved closer and his voice lowered. "We're all we got, remember? You came out here with me for a reason. And I'm going to take care of you."

She brushed him off. "I don't know what it is with men and your insistence that women need to be taken care of. Honestly, I handled everything just fine when I was raising you, didn't I?"

Thomas's gaze darted to Zeke, then back to Agatha. "Well, I've got my phone coming, and I called the bank to get your cards replaced. The company agreed to overnight them and they'll be here tomorrow. Then you won't have to bother Mr. Callahan for anything."

Zeke stiffened. He wanted to take offense at Thomas's assumption. He wasn't being bothered. Spending time with Agatha today had been—interesting, to say the least. But he would have never done it if it wasn't something he was willing to do.

Agatha reached out and touched Zeke's forearm. It was brief and soft, as if a butterfly had landed on him before taking off to find something better. But the motion caught her son's attention and his gaze hardened slightly despite Agatha's reassuring words. "Mr. Callahan was out at the cabin making sure the critters weren't going to be a problem, so I had him take me up to the house to see the damage. After that, he offered to let me tag along when he was headed to town." She lifted the birdhouse. "And look what I got. Isn't it beautiful?"

"Yeah," Thomas mumbled, "it's great."

"You finish up your work here and then come visit me. I'll fix you some dinner and fill you in on what's going to happen next. I don't want to keep you from your work." She shot Zeke a knowing smile. "I'd rather stay on your boss's good side."

Thomas glanced at Zeke once more before nodding. "I'll see you in a few hours, then." He nodded to Zeke. "Thank you, sir, for being so accommodating."

Zeke touched the brim of his hat, then watched the young man go.

Agatha waited until he was out of sight before facing Zeke. "He's a good kid—maybe a little overprotective, but that's how he's always been. It's just been the two of us since he was seven."

"You raised him on your own?" He didn't know why he was surprised. Every chance Agatha got, she made it clear she valued her independence. Why wouldn't she take the task of raising her son all on her own in stride?

She nodded firmly. "His father left us. But what do you expect when a man falls prey to addiction. I found out a few years later he passed away from a drug overdose."

"I'm terribly sorry."

"It was a long time ago." Even as she brushed off his sympathies, she looked away. Something like that had to have made a far larger impact than she was letting on.

She clearly had lived a life that wasn't exactly easy. And yet, here she was, still standing. Anything he might have said would sound terribly cliche. So instead of saying anything, he simply motioned for her to follow him as they continued on their way.

8

———

Agatha

gatha's eyes followed Zeke as he placed her bags on the floor inside the hunting cabin. Everything she'd seen from him up until this point had contradicted what she thought she knew about the man.

From him offering her a free place to stay on his property to taking the time and spending the money to get her new clothing, he'd surprised her at every turn.

He glanced around the cabin as if searching for something, then turned to face her. "If you need anything…"

"I'm perfectly fine. You've done more than enough already," she said lightly. "But thank you for the sentiment."

Zeke removed his cowboy hat and turned it around in his hands. He shifted his weight and let out a heavy breath before laying his gaze on her. "I wanted to make an offer, but after today, I'm not sure how you'd take it."

She wanted to laugh his statement away, but there was

something in the way he said it that made her worry. He'd been so stuck on forcing her to accept his charity. What if he was changing his mind?

Well, if that was the case, she'd figure it out. She always did. Her life had never been easy—a fact she'd gotten used to and one of the biggest reasons she didn't want anyone to feel like they had to take her under their wing. The only one she could count on was herself, and that was made even more clear when her husband had left.

The more time she'd spent with Zeke today, the more she realized her view on things might be a little outdated. This brought her to one unhappy conclusion.

She was already growing accustomed to Zeke's generosity. If he were to rip the rug out from under her, she knew it would hurt more than it should. And she was quickly developing resentment for those feelings. What was taking him so long? Was he waiting for her to give him permission to upend yet another aspect of her life? "Spit it out already."

He lifted a single brow, and she caught yet another glimpse of why people found this man so intimidating.

Agatha ducked her head and tucked a stray strand of hair behind her ear that had fallen from her bun. She cleared her throat but didn't make excuses for her sharp tone. She was the guest, and as such, she should be acting in accordance with that. She could hear Zeke shifting again but kept her gaze trained on the floor.

"I spoke with Tuck at the hardware store today. He thinks he can order the supplies we'll need to fix your house."

Her head snapped up so fast it nearly gave her whiplash. "What?"

A wry smile crossed his face. "We're really going to have to get your hearing checked."

She shook her head and stepped closer to him. "I heard

what you said, but I can't believe it. The contractors—they all said they couldn't—"

"I can get a crew together that is just as good as those contractors. Most of us have experience framing and building barns. Back in my heyday, I helped with several barn raisings."

Agatha's hope dwindled. "This isn't a barn we're talking about. This is my home."

"And it requires similar structural planning. But don't worry. Tuck is a retired builder. He opened his hardware store when he realized he wasn't made for relaxing."

"That sounds like some retirement," Agatha murmured.

"Anyway, I wanted to give you a heads-up that we can put everything into the works. You won't have to stay here very long after all."

So that was it then. Zeke was helping her get her home rebuilt so he could regain control over his cabin. She couldn't blame him. This was his property, and the longer she stayed, the less time he had to spend here. Hunting season would be in a few months, and she was certain he would want to be able to use it.

She smiled brightly, though the joy she should have felt over this news wasn't as great as she'd have imagined it to be. Zeke had figured out how to get her exactly what she wanted. So why did the way he presented it leave a sour taste in her mouth? Perhaps it was the fact she was just now realizing he was a hypocrite. Zeke Callahan wanted to give her something just to get rid of her. Yes, it was generous. But the reasons behind it weren't at all. It just went to show she'd been right about having to look after herself. "Thank you so much. Do you really think you'll be able to find enough help to get this project done quickly?"

"I'm not sure how quickly it'll get done, but it will be faster than waiting on a contractor. I'll give Tuck a call—let him know he's got the green light to put in the order for what we know we'll need right off the bat. Then we can move forward from there."

She swallowed hard, and with that swallow went the disappointment she shouldn't even be feeling. "This is absolutely amazing. Thank you so much. I don't know how I'll ever be able to repay—"

Zeke held up his hand. "Don't worry about that now. We'll see what your insurance covers before we discuss any repayment." With that, he placed his hat on his head and nodded toward her. "Good evening, Ms. Birch. I'll stop by when I have more information." He strode from the cabin, leaving her gaping after him.

A place to stay. Money for clothes. And now a crew to build a house. The contradictory ways in which he was helping her made her head spin. Perhaps she was being too hard on him. Everything he'd done for her up until this point had been to help her. But she still thought he wanted her out. But wouldn't she want the same thing if she were helping someone in a similar situation?

Agatha sighed. She'd just gotten her hopes up that he was as great as she thought him to be. But alas, no one was perfect. She most certainly wasn't, so why even try to put this man on a pedestal?

"Take your hat off at the dinner table. I've taught you better than that." Agatha gave her son a pointed look, but the smile that rested just beneath the surface couldn't be missed.

Thomas removed his hat and placed it on the couch before returning to the small table that could only seat four. He glanced around the hunting cabin with a curiosity befitting a boy half his age.

Agatha chuckled. "I'll give you the grand tour after supper. Why don't you tell me about your day?"

"Why don't you tell me about *yours*?" Thomas scooted his chair in and gave her that look that said he knew something was going on.

Only this time, he was wrong.

"Like I told you before. Zeke took me to the house. Then we went to town. That's all."

"He took you shopping, Mom."

Agatha moved through the small kitchen gathering the dishes and food she'd pulled out for dinner. She didn't meet his gaze nor stop to give him her full attention as there was nothing to discuss, and she could tell where this was heading based on his tone alone. "Not really. I suppose he *took* me there, but he dropped me off so he could run his errands." She hadn't brought up the rebuild yet for this reason. Thomas was naturally inquisitive and often made quick assumptions based on a small amount of data. She didn't need him putting any of those thoughts into her head any more than he was putting them into his own.

"*Mom*."

She placed a casserole dish on the table before taking her seat. "What?"

"What was Mr. Callahan doing out here this morning? I asked around. The wranglers say they don't see him coming and going from his house. He just shows up."

"Maybe he gets up early. You should know that better than anyone. Ranchers are up before light."

"Exactly. I get up before anyone and I don't see him until after breakfast."

"Are you camped out in front of his house?"

"Well, no, but—"

"Then how would you know when he leaves?"

"Is he camped out here?" Thomas shot back at her.

She gave him a stern look, a warning for his tone, and his expression softened.

"Sorry."

"It's fine. No, he's not camped out here. I would have noticed. He came out bright and early to check for animal tracks. It was really rather sweet of him. I'm certain he needed to get up early to do such a thing." She scooped up a serving of the chicken and broccoli casserole and placed it on her plate. "He's really got a strange reputation, you know."

Thomas hadn't moved since taking a seat. His eyes tracked her movements, which only unnerved her further.

"The folks in town say he's harsh and rough. He doesn't let anyone push him around. You said similar things when you got this job a few months ago." She scooped out a serving for him as well, seeing as he didn't get one himself. "Is everyone wrong? Or am I missing something?"

"You're not wrong. Mr. Callahan is strict. He doesn't accept poor behavior. I've seen him fire at least two guys since I started. But he's fair. That's why I like working for him."

Her eyes flitted to meet Thomas's. "So, you like him."

"No, I said I like working for him. Is he a good boss? Sure. I'm learning a lot. But is he someone I would want to spend the day shopping with? No."

"Oh, for heaven's sake. It wasn't like we were on a date or anything." There, she'd said it. That was what she knew her son was getting at. This was how it always was when there was another man in her life. Even a man who didn't mean anything but a roof over her head.

"Wasn't it? Because it sure sounded like a date to me."

Agatha rolled her eyes with a laugh and motioned toward the food on his plate. "Eat up. There's nothing to be concerned about. In fact, I found out something you might be pleased with."

Thomas picked up his fork and scooped up a bite of the

casserole. His eyes locked with hers, but he didn't say anything. He looked so much like his father—the parts of him that she'd loved dearly.

"Mr. Callahan has some connections in town. He said he can get a crew together to rebuild our home."

Thomas's fork stopped mid-air before it even reached his lips. His mouth hung open, and for a moment, time itself froze. Then he put the fork down. "What are you saying? Zeke Callahan is going to build our house back?"

"See? Everything you thought isn't even an issue."

"What do you mean? A guy doesn't just do something like that. What happened between the two of you? Should I be worried?"

"Calm down, Thomas. He wants me out of his cabin. That's what this is all about. The contractors are at least a year out, but there are no vacancies anywhere close. I moved out this way to spend time with you, so I'm not moving to Colorado Springs while we figure this out."

"Have you talked to Shane?"

"No, I haven't had a chance."

"Mom! He's your boss."

"And I don't have to be back to work until tomorrow. I've had a lot on my mind lately, or have you forgotten?" Agatha could feel her temper rising. She didn't have to explain herself to her son, and he was quickly forgetting his place.

"I'm sure if you talked to Shane, he'd be able to help you find something. He's got all that housing—"

"Yes, housing for veterans and families with children who have disabilities. How would it look if he booted one of them out for his PR manager? I can tell you how that would go over with the press. Not very good at all. After that whole fiasco with his cousins, he needed me to come in here and make sure that people didn't lose their trust in his businesses. I'm not about to be the cog that comes loose in this whole thing."

Thomas settled back in his seat. "You're sure nothing is going on?"

She laughed if only to stop herself from dwelling on that strange sense of sadness she'd felt over finding out Zeke's true intentions. "Yes. I'm absolutely certain. Zeke is the kind of guy who likes his privacy. If he wanted me to stay, he wouldn't have found a way to get me out of here sooner."

Her son frowned, staring at his plate of food. "Yeah, okay. I guess you're right."

She leaned forward, placing her hand against his cheek. "Of course I'm right. We were lucky he was willing to let me stay in the first place. Now, let's not look a gift horse in the mouth. In a few days I'll know approximately when the building will start. I'm sure Zeke will ask some of his wranglers to help out. Would you be interested?"

He shrugged. "Actually, Adeline has sorta taken a shine to me. She says I'm a natural with the horses. She wants me to shadow her and learn what I can. I'd like to learn how to train them like the professionals do."

Agatha shifted her hand to his and gave it a squeeze. "Then you do that. I'll be overseeing the house, and you can come for dinner any time you'd like."

"Anytime? I'm coming every night. The food at the ranch isn't as good as the stuff my mother makes," Thomas said.

Agatha smiled, warmed by the compliment while also knowing there was a deeper meaning to his need to spend the evenings with her. It wasn't that he was so attached to her he couldn't leave her side. On the contrary, he was fiercely independent. But he still loved his mother, and he wanted to make sure she was okay.

She saw nothing wrong with that. As long as he didn't overstep and start bossing her around. Agatha was her own person, and she wasn't going to yield to anyone. Not her ex. Not her son. And definitely not the man who insisted on helping her.

They would all just have to accept that she was as wild as any of those mustangs roaming free in the more uninhabited parts of the West.

Thomas picked up his fork and dug into his meal, leaving her to her own thoughts—most of which concerned none other than Zeke Callahan.

9

Zeke

Birds chirped in nearby trees despite the sound of the hammers and nail guns that made the most intolerable racket. It wouldn't have been so bad if Zeke hadn't been kept up all hours with every last sound he heard in the underbrush.

What else did he expect when he was stuck in a tent not even twenty yards from the cabin he should have been staying in? He wasn't sour about the fact that Agatha was staying in his second home. On the contrary, he wouldn't have had it any other way. At least there, he could keep an eye on her.

There was no telling the kinds of people there were out in the world who might do her harm. Copper Creek was small enough, but if she'd ended up moving to Colorado Springs in the interim, she most definitely had a higher chance of getting hurt.

Zeke wandered along the exterior of the house. Over the month or so, the entire interior had been gutted, stripped of all the Birch belongings and furniture. Agatha had insisted on saving as much as she could, but being the skeptic he was, he didn't have much hope for her.

Still, she was planning on sending whatever she could to a specialty cleaner in the city.

Now, they were left with removing the damaged wood siding and reframing what had sat beneath it. That was what they worked on today. Wood, both charred and new, lay scattered along the property. There were about a dozen men working today, more than he'd expected for this kind of work.

Zeke stopped for a moment to admire how the community had come together to aid in putting this woman's home back to rights.

"I don't know how you did it, but we're going to get this thing framed in one day." Tuck sidled up next to Zeke, but his gaze was on the clipboard in front of him. "I've never seen so many willing men."

Zeke chuckled. "Well, I have seven daughters and one girl I call daughter. Their husbands know better than to tell their father-in-law no."

Tuck chuckled, his raspy voice louder than Zeke had ever heard it. "I suppose you make a good point." He glanced around the area, his brows furrowing. "Isn't Shane Owens one of those husbands you were referring to?"

Zeke nodded. "Mr. Owens took a trip to California two days ago. Something to do with family matters. He said he'd help when he gets back, though I don't know if there's much he'd be capable of." He gave Tuck a knowing look. The city folk around here could pretend all they wanted that they could do what the locals did, but it didn't make it true.

His friend seemed to understand exactly what he was referring to. He didn't make any further comment about Shane's absence or what they might assign him to when he returned. Instead, he gestured toward the back side of the house. "With the damage being localized back here, the structure didn't need as much work as we were expecting. I'd like to redo all the siding, though. It'd be a good idea to upgrade for insulation purposes."

Zeke's eyes followed Tuck's motion. "I think you're right. Ms. Birch would probably appreciate that. I'll make sure to tell her when I see her."

"That might be sooner than you think."

Zeke shot a confused look at Tuck, only to find the man staring off in another direction. He followed Tuck's gaze to find Agatha wandering through the construction zone. "What in the Sam Hill is she doing?" Zeke muttered as he charged forward, not waiting for Tuck to respond.

The woman should know better than to be hanging around right now. He'd left her at the cabin for a reason. On purpose, he hadn't even knocked on her door to tell her he was heading out.

She had her hands behind her back, and she was wearing those ridiculous-looking overalls. At least this time she was wearing sensible shoes.

Zeke took the steps two at a time up the back porch and skidded to a stop right beside her. Agatha glanced at him, surprise not even registering. "Oh, good morning, Zeke. I didn't realize you were starting today until my son called."

"Your son—Tom called you?"

Agatha crossed her arms. Even with all the chaos and building going on around her, she was able to take his full attention hostage with one look. She stared up at him with shrewd eyes. "Why didn't you tell me we were starting today?"

"*We*?" he stammered. "There is no *we* in this. I don't want you anywhere near this site while we're working with heavy machinery."

One single brow lifted before a smirk touched her lips. "Heavy machinery?"

"Yes," he blustered, gesturing toward the equipment that allowed him to run the nail guns the men were using. Not only that, but they had saws and other tools she was bound to get hurt on. "If you get injured while you're here, I'm going to be liable."

Her hands moved to her hips. "How do you figure that?"

"Because..." He didn't have an answer for that. This whole situation was being done charitably. The men understood that. He had the workers added to his business's liability insurance, but that didn't include Agatha. "Well, because I'm in charge."

She took a step closer, not seeming to be aware that several of the men working—mostly the men who were involved with his daughters—had stopped their work to watch this conversation play out. She scooped up a hammer and twirled it around in her hand. "I wouldn't consider this heavy machinery, would you?"

"No, but—"

"And as far as the saws and nail guns go... I'm not a child, Zeke. I can take care of myself. I'm not going to pick up and play with any of this stuff. I will, however, stay on-site while the work is taking place so I can make sure that nothing goes wrong."

Zeke let out a bark of laughter. "I'm sorry, but do you have any experience with building?"

"Of course not."

"Then how in heaven's name do you suppose you're going to ensure nothing goes wrong?" He'd got her there. The argument would be settled, and she'd be forced to go home with her tail between her legs.

"Because I have a knack for details. For instance, I believe most contractors maintain a much cleaner workspace. The new wood is lying around in heaps among the stuff that's been damaged. Are you making sure your men keep it separate?"

"They're doing just fine the way they are. We can tell what's damaged and what isn't."

"Perhaps you can, but I don't think some of these men can. Just a moment ago, I pointed out a piece that needed to be removed. There were some issues with it."

Zeke's head snapped up as if just by her notifying him of this problem, he'd be able to find the piece and the person responsible for making a liar out of him. Of course he couldn't, so he brought his eyes back to Agatha. "I'll have them clean up the area. Is that good enough? Then will you leave?"

She shook her head. He didn't know why he'd counted on her listening. He'd nearly forgotten just how stubborn she could be. The way she stood in front of him like she was going up against a bear. He might as well have been one with the way he puffed out his chest and scowled at her.

"You need to leave, Ms. Birch."

"I'll do no such thing. This is my home, and I'm allowed to be here. I might not be able to help with the framing, but I'm sure I can be of use in some other way. There's patching and caulking—even running to get materials for the men working."

He groaned, dragging a hand down his face. "There's nothing I can do to convince you to leave, is there?"

"Something tells me you already know the answer to that question. Now, if you'll excuse me, I'm going to continue checking everything out. Don't worry, I'll stay out of the way." She moved away from him.

Zeke couldn't keep his mouth shut as his eyes followed her. "Don't get hurt."

She stopped right where she was, then turned to face him. The expression on her face could only be described as that of a lioness in the wild. "I'm not some damsel in distress, Mr. Callahan. Stop treating me as such and we'll get along just fine."

Several chuckles rippled through the group of men working, but with one dark look from Zeke, it stopped. Great. Now he had to worry about this job getting done right and the safety of one very stubborn woman.

This could be the hardest few months of his life.

WITH THE FRAMING DONE, the next thing they worked on was the exterior siding and the interior sheetrocking. Zeke was still struggling to get enough sleep. Each and every day that Agatha turned up, his blood pressure rose. If she wasn't wandering into an area where something might fall on her, she was picking up a sharp or dangerous tool. The side-eyed stares he'd gotten from everyone, including Shane, only added to his foul mood.

It didn't matter if he brought Agatha on the ATV or not. She always managed to find her way to the house. While everyone else said how amazing and sweet she was, all he saw was her smug smile. She knew what she was doing, and it was infuriating.

He grabbed a large piece of siding and placed it against the house, holding it steady with his knee before he grabbed a nearby nail gun. At least right now, she was inside bothering the guys who were putting the insulation into the wall. Her laughter raked against his nerves in a way that both irritated him and made him want to hear more.

Apparently, Agatha was the kind of woman who could get along with everyone. Not one individual at the site had anything bad to say about her.

He marched over to the stack of siding and grabbed another long panel. His fingers slipped as he lifted it, and at that exact moment, Agatha walked past him. If she'd been just a few feet to the right, she would have been knocked to her behind.

Agatha gasped, jumping back, but it didn't matter. Zeke was already at odds with all of this. He let the panel drop to his feet and set a fiery gaze on the woman.

"Just because you're comfortable around everything that's going on doesn't mean you should be on site."

Her eyes widened but only slightly. It was as if she were more surprised by his talking to her than she was over nearly losing a limb.

Zeke let out a sharp breath before he removed his hat and threw it to the ground. He raked his hand through his hair, if only to keep it steady. "What did I tell you? This isn't the place for someone like you."

"Someone like me?" she said flatly.

"Exactly someone like you. Or did you not notice that you could have been seriously maimed?"

Her mouth quirked upward slightly. "You're being ridiculous."

"No, I'm thinking logically. You don't wear a helmet—"

"Neither do most of your men."

This was a losing battle. Not even the risk of being hurt was enough to sway this woman. Zeke threw his hands into the air and stormed off, leaving the men who were still working behind. His heart beat even harder in his chest and he clutched at it with shaking hands. The more distance he put between himself and the situation, the more he realized he'd overreacted, but he wasn't about to go back there and tell her as much.

Something had to change one way or another. She couldn't just wander the construction site when she didn't have experience—and yet she couldn't see things from his side.

By the time he made it back to the cabin, he still wasn't ready to head back to her house and get back to work. Once upon a time, he'd been in control of everything. He could say a single word and people would fall in line.

What happened?

Perhaps taking the afternoon off would be just the thing to give him some clarity.

ZEKE TRUDGED through the woods near his tent. The early morning light filled the sky with a navy-blue color. When the sun came up all the way, it would be a beautiful day. Already he couldn't see a cloud in the sky.

He wandered along the trail that would lead him toward the cabin where he had parked the ATV. If he headed out to the house early enough, maybe he could catch up on some of the stuff he hadn't completed the day before.

That was one thing he hated. He'd wasted time with his little temper tantrum, and he wasn't about to let the men working point it out.

Dew collected on the tall grasses. Birds chirped. Even the rustling of the critters in the underbrush had begun. His sharp eyes kept a lookout for any tracks that might look problematic. If there was even one paw-print that was large enough to draw attention, he would have to postpone heading out to the house.

Thankfully, there wasn't anything that he could see.

Zeke took a deep breath, inhaling the scent of pine and dirt. Evelyn had helped him see that doing so would ground him, help him find his center.

She wasn't wrong.

In the early morning, that was when he could find peace. It didn't matter what had happened the day before. Today was a new day.

He rounded a large bush, intending on getting to the ATV that was parked in the back but instead found Agatha. She stood in front of it, dressed and wearing a jacket, with hands on her hips. She frowned at the ATV, her fury giving him a small amount of satisfaction. Whatever she was upset about, she probably deserved it.

Zeke moved closer to her, and she must have noticed him out of the corner of her eye because she let out a yelp and jumped backward. Her eyes widened, then narrowed, and she pointed an accusatory finger at him.

"What are you doing here?" she said.

"I beg your pardon?"

She gestured angrily at the ATV. "Are you spying on me?"

He laughed. That wasn't something he'd expected her to say. "I'm sorry, ma'am, but spying on you is not something I have any time for."

"Then why is that here? Why are you here?" The accusation and suspicion in her voice were almost as amusing as the glare she'd set on the vehicle when he'd arrived. "I told you I don't need a babysitter."

He slowed until he stopped about ten yards from her. His arms were crossed over his chest and the amusement had fallen from his face. "Sorry to break this to you, but there are more important things to do than to hover outside of your residence. I don't owe you anything, by the way."

Her stubbornness remained, but now she tapped her foot. He wouldn't have been at all surprised if she blocked his path when he climbed on the back of the ATV.

Zeke blew out a resigned sigh. "You're not going to let me leave without an answer, are you?"

"You're right about that."

"Fine. Follow me."

10

———

Agatha

Agatha hadn't expected to see the ATV outside the back window when she'd gotten up. Granted, she'd never been up this early since she'd moved into the hunting cabin. But seeing it there had given her a start, and now she was fuming.

Zeke disappeared behind a large shrub. It was still too dark for her to see much, and when he slipped away from the light on the back of the cabin, she couldn't help but hesitate. It wasn't that she was scared he'd hurt her. If anything, Zeke was a little overprotective.

She only had a few seconds to wonder what could possibly prompt him to drag her into the woods this early in the morning. Agatha stared down at the boots she'd slipped on before sneaking out to get a better look at the ATV, then she groaned and tromped after Zeke.

There was a flash of his hat before he went around a curve in a trail she hadn't even realized was back here. Her steps quickened. If she got lost in the woods, then she really would be eating her words. She couldn't afford to get hurt while on his property or he would force her to stay cooped up like some primped princess.

Agatha took one more turn and completely collided with Zeke.

He stumbled forward a step, and she grunted in a very unladylike way. Zeke turned to face her. Was that a smirk he wore on his face? Boy, what she wouldn't give to wipe it clean off. Agatha glared at him but still muttered, "Sorry."

Zeke stared at her expectantly.

"What? I said I was sorry. Do you want me to do more?" It was far too early to be getting bossed around by Zeke Callahan.

He jutted his chin to her left. "That's what."

She glanced over her shoulder, suddenly realizing a tent had been set up. It was a deep forest green color and small. She wasn't even sure she would have noticed it if she'd been wandering along the trails on her own in full daylight.

Agatha thumbed toward it. "Whose is that?"

"Mine."

"Yours."

He nodded.

"I'm trying not to overreact, but it really feels like you set up that tent so you could keep an eye on me."

Zeke worked his jaw. He didn't look thrilled about being caught, but then why would he? No one liked to get caught doing something they shouldn't. His eyes flitted to meet hers, then a puff of air released from his lips. "That's not it at all."

"Really? Then what is it?"

He shoved his hands in his pockets and put all his weight on one boot. Zeke didn't look at her. Instead, he glanced up to the sky, then at the tree line—anywhere but directly at her. "I moved out to the tent after the fire."

"Again, you're not making a good case for yourself." She

shifted uncomfortably. There was something strange about the way he avoided telling her what this was about. "Just tell me what's going on."

He tilted his head, glancing at her from a strange angle like his confession was almost painful. "I was staying in the cabin when your house caught fire."

At first Agatha didn't grasp what he'd said. He was staying in the cabin? Wait. *Her* cabin? "You were staying here?"

He wore a crooked sort of grin, though it looked more like he was smiling out of self-preservation rather than amusement. "Yeah."

So many questions popped into her head as she stared at the tent that wouldn't be able to hold more than one person, and that was stretching it. The only question that got past her lips was one word. "Why?"

"*Why?*"

"Why are you staying out here? Don't forget that I've seen your house. Are you seriously trying to convince me that you would rather sleep on the cold, hard ground instead of the bed I know you have at home?"

What was left of his smile fled from his face and his eyes flickered with wariness. "I don't think it's any of your business where I choose to sleep."

She flushed at his statement. That wasn't what she was trying to get at. She wanted to know what was keeping him from staying with his family—in a home that was definitely more comfortable than living in the wilderness. Agatha didn't get a chance to backtrack before Zeke continued.

"I'm staying out here because my home is a little crowded with so many people coming and going. And when it's not chaos, it's just too... quiet."

As much as she would have loved to point out that his statements were completely contradictory, she couldn't. There was something in the tone of his voice that tugged at her, pulling her under as if she'd been dragged down by an undertow.

Much like one of her first days in town after the fire, gossip was rampant. She'd heard everything there was to know about Zeke Callahan before she'd had the pleasure of meeting him. His wife passed when the girls were young. The rules of his household were so strict he probably should have been born and raised his family in a time period that was centuries before this one. He was hard but fair when it came to everything business related, and he shielded what was his with every ounce of strength that he possessed—making him incredibly protective.

Along with all of that, she had heard he hadn't dated anyone since he'd lost his wife. She'd overheard that, at one time, they'd thought Zeke would end up with someone named Liz, but clearly that hadn't happened.

For the first time since she'd met Zeke, she was looking at him in a different light. He had spent his entire life in control of everything he could. And now his daughters were growing up and moving out. His wife wasn't there to fill in the holes.

Was it possible he was out here because he was lonely?

The thought was almost laughable. Just because he'd opted to stay in a tent while she was using his cabin didn't mean he was interested in *her* company. He'd said so himself that he'd been staying out here since before the fire.

Oh, how swiftly her heart could be manipulated into feeling something that wasn't there. First, she'd thought he might want her to stay longer, but then he went out of his way to help rebuild her home.

Now she had nearly made herself believe he wanted to spend extra time with her. If yesterday's events had taught her anything, it was that Zeke wasn't interested in spending even a spare second with her.

It wasn't likely he was even remotely lonely enough to put himself through such torture.

"Okay, you can stop looking at me like that. I'm not some poor soul you need to save," he ground out. "There are plenty of reasons I stay out here. Some have to do with my family, and the others have to do with getting your house done."

There it was. The proof she needed. Zeke wanted her gone. It was time to protect her heart from going rogue, lest she lose a piece of it to this man who was rougher around the edges than a cactus.

Agatha pulled her jacket tighter around herself. "I wasn't looking at you in any particular way."

"Yeah, sure. Then why did your eyes seem to glisten like you were about to cry? Look, I'm a grown man with my own problems. I don't need you adding to them and making me feel like…" He sighed. "Just know that I'm camping out here for now, and it's my own business what I do with my personal time, alright?" With that, he stormed out of the clearing and back down the trail.

The sun had risen a little more, turning the sky into a pretty orange color. It was easier to make her way along the trail and not worry about falling on her face, especially when Zeke used his long strides.

She wanted to say something to make him feel better, but she was at a complete loss for words. Anything she might say could set him off, and that was the exact opposite of what she wanted to do.

So she blurted the one thing that came to mind, then instantly regretted it. "Would you like to stay for breakfast?"

Zeke had made it to the ATV and was quickly preparing it for the ride. When she spoke, he froze. Even with his back to her, she could tell he wasn't sure about accepting.

There was no reason for Zeke to want to stay. He could barely stand her. Unfortunately for him, she'd been raised right and she wasn't going to take no for an answer. "You know, everyone needs to eat, and from the look of that campsite, it didn't look like you cooked anything. I didn't even see a fire—but then I guess that would make sense. How else would you have hidden the spy camp you'd set up?"

Agatha bit back a grin, fighting a small bout of laughter.

It became even harder to do so when Zeke spun around to face her, his eyes shooting daggers at her. Luckily, he caught sight of just how bad she was at hiding her teasing, and his expression sobered. He peered at her, the anger fading to confusion, then curiosity. "You want me to stay for breakfast? Like a date?"

She held up her hands, a nervous laugh spilling from her lips. "Oh, no. Definitely not a date. I just figured... since you were already here and I was getting ready to fix something... you'd like to eat, too. The food *is* yours, is it not?"

"Technically, I suppose it is."

She jerked her chin toward the house. "Then let me fix you something. It's the least I could do considering everything you've done for me thus far." Agatha didn't wait for a response before she hurried inside.

Every nerve in her body was antsy. There was nothing about her mental state that was normal. And for what? A man who didn't even like her? She needed to shut down that thought process before it turned even more dangerous.

It had been far too easy to empathize with the man. That was where her problems started. It would be wise to keep her distance from this point forward—as much as someone could, given the situation.

The back door banged open, then closed, and she jumped.

Right, she'd invited him for breakfast.

Why had she *done* that?

Agatha placed both her cool hands on her flushed cheeks as she faced the window in the kitchen. She could hear the heavy footfalls of his boots as he made his way from the mudroom toward the kitchen.

The second he entered the main living space, she set to work. Eggs. Bacon. Toast. She gathered everything she needed and prepared a quick breakfast that any cowboy would be happy to eat.

But the second she sat across from him at the kitchen table, she immediately regretted her decision—just not for the reasons she would have thought.

Zeke's demeanor had changed from the stiff, guarded cowboy outside to someone entirely different before her. He'd removed his hat and placed it on a hook near the door. His hair was mussed, but in a way that made her itch to run her fingers through it in order to tidy it up.

It was his eyes that drew her focus the most.

They were kind—the sort of eyes that made her feel... safe.

He lifted a brow, and that was when she realized she was staring. Shoot! Agatha wasn't doing a very good job at keeping her feelings locked away. She fixed him a plate, then set her focus on her food.

Their meal continued like that—in complete silence. Alone in her head with her thoughts, Agatha returned to what she'd been going over when they were out by the tent. If a man spent the last decade or so completely alone except for his daughters, he had to be struggling with his self-identity.

Hadn't she done the same when she found herself single and raising her son on her own? It was incredibly difficult to shift from one mentality to another.

Well, bother! Why did she have to empathize so fully with him? It would have been so much easier to keep him at arm's length during the rest of this process.

Something in her heart told her that wasn't the plan. There were reasons certain people walked into each other's lives, and this could be the very one why their paths had crossed. Zeke needed someone to show him how to find himself again.

Zeke motioned toward a small vase she'd displayed on the

table. It held a few wildflowers from a walk she'd taken on the way back from her place the other day. The flowers were already looking a little shabby. She just hadn't gotten to the point of replacing them.

Agatha waited for Zeke to make a comment regarding her stealing from him. But he didn't. He swallowed his food and finally commented on it. "You like flowers."

She let out a strangled laugh. "Of course I do. What woman doesn't?"

"Oh, you'd be surprised at what some women despise out here. Most of the rancher's wives tend to think that flowers are best kept in the ground."

Well, there it was. The statement she'd been expecting. He didn't want her to pluck flowers from his property. "Look, I didn't know—"

"Evelyn—my wife—she loved flowers, too. She'd make me buy them from town every single time I went." The sadness crept into her chest, making everything turn cold. Zeke lifted his gaze to meet hers. "I think I would have preferred something like this, though. It's a lot simpler." He picked up his napkin and wiped his mouth. Then he took his dishes to the sink.

She followed suit, making sure to rinse the dishes so they'd be easier to do when she got back from her house.

Then Zeke caught her off guard again. He took the dish from her hand, his fingers grazing hers, and washed every dish currently in the sink. Agatha only came to her senses when he handed the first one to her expectantly.

She yanked a dish towel from the counter and dried it without a word. They worked in companionable silence, neither one speaking. Discussing what the day held would likely end up in an argument, so Agatha was perfectly fine to keep her thoughts to herself. The walk to the construction site wasn't something she was particularly excited for, but it was necessary if she planned on being there every day. When she was done, she headed for the front door but then stopped in her tracks.

Somehow Zeke had made it to the door without her realizing. He stood there, his arms crossed, as he leaned against the door like he had all the time in the world. "I don't figure I could convince you to stay put today." At least his voice was lighter this time, almost tender.

"Nope."

"I didn't think so." He pulled away from the door, opened it, and gestured for her to leave first. "Care for a ride?"

11

———

Zeke

Something strange happened between the time when Zeke showed Agatha the tent and the moment they got onto the ATV. Zeke would like to have said that it had occurred when he bore his soul to her—telling her things he would have never told his daughters.

And perhaps that was part of it, only it didn't help him understand why spending breakfast with her had felt so good. Nor did it explain why a billowing of heat seared the organs in his chest when they touched.

The brush of his skin against hers had been unintentional, and yet it had left a lasting impact. Now, he was dealing with a similar problem.

Agatha's arms were around his middle, holding on as if her life depended on it—and part of him wanted to push the speed of the ATV to the limit just so she would hold on to him that much tighter.

He couldn't help but enjoy the way she clung to him, reminding him very much that he was still a man who wanted to share his life with someone. There was just one big problem.

She most definitely wasn't his type.

Up until this point, they'd butted heads. She had an attitude. Nothing was worth dealing with that. Agatha was one of those women who was single for a reason, and he knew exactly what that reason was.

Unfortunately, his heart and his body didn't care about that. His heart seemed to thrum with a nervous energy, and for what? Some woman he'd met several weeks ago?

Nope.

That wasn't going to happen. He was just having an off couple of weeks. All of this would blow over after the house got done.

Zeke continued to remind himself of this the rest of the ride to the house. And when they arrived, he practically launched himself from the ATV and toward the building. The exterior looked just about done. All it needed was a fresh coat of paint. Thankfully, the men he'd enlisted were the kind who got work done.

He didn't bother keeping an eye on Agatha. Wherever she was going to go, she'd do so with or without his permission. It would be best if he were to just throw himself into the work that needed to be done so he could get his mind off her and the feelings she had elicited.

"Nice of you to show up." Tuck pulled away from Sean and Riley, a coffee in hand. "After the way you left yesterday, we didn't know if you'd be back."

"What are you talking about, Tuck? This is my project."

"And you seem to be having the hardest time getting along with the one person you're doing this for."

"She's the one who's being difficult," Zeke said, low enough that only Tuck could hear him. "She doesn't even bother staying safe when she's here."

Tuck chuckled as they wandered through the kitchen that was now getting taped and mudded. "It's not like this place is as dangerous as you're making it out to be. It's a house. Are we using tools? Sure. But it's nothing I wouldn't let my daughters use if they wanted to do a remodel."

Zeke stopped to look at his friend, raising one eyebrow as he stared at the man. "You would let your daughters use a table saw? Because I can tell you one thing. I wouldn't let my daughters touch one with a ten-foot pole."

"It's not so different than riding a horse." Again, Tuck chuckled.

The fire in Zeke's stomach rolled with indignation. "That's *completely* different. Riding a horse when one has been raised in the saddle is something expected. But for someone who doesn't know the business end of a saw... well, they have no reason to be here in the first place. Agatha Birch is one such woman. At any moment she could—"

Tuck's eyes darted to one side, then right back to Zeke, but it was too late to stop himself even after seeing Tuck's subtle shake of his head.

Zeke froze. Agatha was right behind him. It wasn't until that moment he could feel her presence, but now that he did, it was overwhelming. Why hadn't Tuck said something, for Pete's sake?

Slowly, he turned around and faced the woman who he knew would be glaring at him.

Surprisingly enough, Agatha simply gazed at him with an unreadable expression. Tuck shifted, then ducked out of the room, mumbling something about a delivery coming.

Agatha crossed her arms, her head tilting with a bit of curiosity. "You don't think I can handle myself."

Zeke had to snap his mouth shut in order to prevent himself from saying something really stupid. He'd been saying as much all this time. What did she think he was referring to?

"Well, you're wrong. Just because you don't know something doesn't mean you can't learn. It doesn't matter how old you are. An old dog can learn new tricks."

He huffed but still stopped himself from uttering a word.

"And I'll have you know that you hired one such person. Before Slate Rock Ranch, my son had never worked with horses. He's got a natural talent, that's all."

Zeke lifted his brows. Granted, he hadn't been the one to hire the boy, but finding out that he had someone working for him who hadn't grown up in this world unsettled him to a small degree.

Agatha moved closer still. "Tell you what. If at any point I get even a paper cut, I'll leave you and this whole project alone."

Quiet laughter came from another room. Zeke couldn't tell if the men were reacting to her statement or to how they expected him to reply. This offer was what he'd needed to get her out from underfoot. But now that she was making the offer, he wasn't sure he wanted it to go down that way. A papercut was nothing. He wanted to be *right*.

She was making him out to be an overbearing fool, a label he'd worked hard to move away from.

Zeke sliced a hand through the air, dismissing her. "I will never admit that you belong here when you have no business being on site. But I'm done pushing you to leave. You're going to do what you're going to do, right?"

He wasn't certain, but he thought there might have been a hint of a smile that touched her lips. She lifted her chin, a movement that suited her stubborn nature. "Okay, then."

No argument. No insistence that she was going to follow her

plan. No humility. He didn't know why he expected anything different. This was a woman who had gotten her way much of her life. There was no way she would back down.

Perhaps he should have shaken her hand regarding her offer just so he could get some semblance of peace. At least then he had a guarantee for when something inevitably went wrong.

Even as the most annoying woman he had ever met stood a few feet from him, his body was still reacting as though she was someone he wanted to get to know better—someone he was drawn to.

Zeke swallowed hard and inched away from her. Was there actually something about her confidence and stubbornness he found attractive? That couldn't be right. Evelyn wasn't like that at all. She was quiet and strong but not stubborn like a mule.

He gave his head a sharp shake and turned away from her, but she stopped him. "Mr. Callahan?"

Frozen in his place, his back to her, he waited for her to speak. Her use of his last name was usually reserved for when she wanted to put additional distance between them—something that also indicated she was irritated with him. Well, she could join the party. This morning had been a blunder from the moment she caught him outside the cabin to the confusion over how being near her made him feel.

"I wanted to..." She made a disgruntled sound, something that made him want to smile though he knew he needed to keep a straight face. "I need to thank you."

Without facing her, he said, "You've thanked me already."

"I know, but I don't think you realize just how much this means to me. You've single-handedly helped me find a place to stay and got the repairs on my home started. I know you're a busy man, and yet you're... going out of your way..." Her voice trailed off.

"You're welcome," he said, trying to keep any emotion out of his voice.

"I don't understand it."

He turned then. "Don't understand what?"

"Why you're helping me. It's not... something..." Her face flushed, and for the first time he saw a side of her he hadn't before. The walls were down; she wasn't confident or stubborn. Nor was she distraught and in pain. If anything, she was wary, like a lost woodland creature who got cornered by a hunter. There was something in her countenance that made him want to move closer, but he refused. Agatha shifted her weight, and her arms dropped so she could clasp her hands together. The wringing motion drew his attention.

Much like the evening when he'd held her while she cried, he felt this uncontrollable desire to wrap her up in his arms and protect her from everything and everyone who might wish her harm.

"Why are you helping me?" she blurted in a whisper, her blush even brighter. "I overheard a couple of the men talking. They seem to think there's something going on between us."

He blinked, the haze disappearing. Her words were like a punch to the gut, made all the more painful by the emotions he'd been experiencing against his will. Was this yet another sign he needed to get back out there? Could Evelyn be telling him he needed to find someone so he didn't remain alone? "That's ridiculous," he muttered. "A piece of advice. The men here gossip almost worse than the women do. I'm helping you because it's the right thing to do." Zeke rubbed the back of his neck and peered at her, his continence softening. "It's a welcome distraction even if the person I'm helping is as hard-headed as you."

A hint of a smile touched her lips and she looked away. "I'll try not to be so hard-headed."

The chuckle that left his lips surprised even himself. "I

wouldn't dream of changing a thing about you." There was a logical part of him that knew she wasn't his type. That same part was what helped him keep his distance. At the same time, he couldn't deny that he saw a little bit of his second daughter in her. Brielle had the confidence and stubbornness that had him pulling out his hair, and yet he loved her even more for it.

Agatha peered at him, a funny look crossing her face. She offered him a small smile and gestured toward the stairs that had been framed in. "I'm going to help upstairs, then. I hear they won't be using a table saw up there."

He watched her, unmoving until she disappeared, then he raked a hand through his hair and blew out a long breath. Something crunched into the floor on the other side of the room, and his head snapped up to find Wade wandering into the kitchen from the living room. He had a rag in his hands as he wiped them clean.

Zeke frowned at him. What were the chances he was one of the men contributing to the gossip Agatha had mentioned? How much had he heard of their conversation?

Wade leaned against the doorjamb casually, his features guarded. There was something in his eyes that made it clear he'd heard every last second of Zeke's conversation with Agatha, and he was amused, to say the least.

Zeke's gaze hardened. "Just because you married my daughter doesn't mean you get to come in here and—"

The young man lifted his hands and brows at the same time. "I'm not coming in here to do a single thing. But you should know some of the guys think you have a thing for Ms. Birch."

"Yeah, I gathered as much," Zeke said, not sure where this was going.

"Brielle will be thrilled."

Zeke shot a surprised look at his newest son-in-law.

Wade chuckled. "She's been saying how you'd be a lot easier to get along with if you'd just get married again."

He snorted as Wade tossed the rag onto his shoulder.

"In fact, Bri was planning on setting you up with someone one town over. She thought you might need a distraction."

Zeke met Wade's eyes. "She was?" That might actually be just the thing to solve this strange feeling he was experiencing. He needed to get this desire for Ms. Agatha Birch out of his system before it became a problem.

"Yeah, but it seems like you have your sights set on someone else."

"Tell her to set it up."

The surprise on Wade's face would have been comical if it wasn't for the weight that Zeke felt in this very moment. He needed to get his mind off Agatha. Not only would it be a bad idea because they weren't compatible, there were other unpleasant implications—one of which being she was the mother of someone who worked for him.

"Are you sure about that?"

"I asked, didn't I?" Zeke's voice was gruff and short. "If Brielle thinks there's someone I might get along with, then have her set it up. I'm available in the evenings. I just need to know where and when." Maybe he'd be able to finally get this woman out of his head. He picked up a bucket of spackle and a scraper to start sealing in the nails, choosing to avoid looking at Wade, praying he'd get the hint and leave. Thankfully, he did just that a few moments later, leaving him alone with his thoughts of women.

Not just women in general.

One woman.

Agatha Birch.

Things were so much simpler when he was alone in the cabin. Thinking about it, he realized this had all started when the girls reached marriage age. If he could just go back in time to when it was easy, he wouldn't be dealing with any of this.

When he was younger, he might have considered dating someone like Agatha. But he wasn't young anymore, and just the thought of going toe-to-toe with her made him feel utterly exhausted.

He sent a prayerful request heavenward that this woman Brielle found would be just the thing to push Agatha out of his mind and help him get back to when his life was simple.

12

———

Agatha

gatha stared out the back window of the cabin every morning. And every morning she was a little more excited to see the ATV waiting for her.

Okay, it wasn't waiting for her. It was waiting for Zeke. But since that first morning she'd caught him, he'd continued to drive her to the house. They hadn't shared breakfast again after that morning, but today she planned on inviting him again.

Since the moment he'd said he wouldn't change a thing about her, she couldn't get the words out of her head.

That, coupled with realizing he was helping her just to help her, had triggered something deeper inside her. Zeke was just as good a guy as he made himself out to be. He was misunderstood at times, and she'd been guilty of doing just that. But now that she knew she'd pegged him all wrong, the knots in her stomach kept on twisting tighter and tighter.

Her eyes kept a shrewd watch on the ATV. If he waited

much longer, then they wouldn't have much time to eat. She probably needed to head out there and find him.

The sun had come up enough to light her way. It shouldn't be too hard to locate him. Agatha nodded resolutely. That was exactly what she was going to do. She'd track him down and make a standing offer for him to join her for breakfast as long as he was staying in the tent.

She grabbed her jacket and headed out in the oversized boots around the side of the house and along the trail.

Birds chirped and critters scuttled beneath the brush. Each step she took, a twig or something else crushed beneath her boot. It smelled like rain, though she hadn't seen any in a while. Pine was another smell that inundated her senses.

Where her house was located, she didn't have access to nature like this. Her property had been gutted of all the natural beauty she had here. Granted, it was a smaller property and the owners likely wanted to have a yard for their children to play in. She couldn't fault them for that. When she was raising Thomas, she would have wanted the same, only they were stuck in their city apartment for most of his childhood. At the time she would have given anything to move her son out to the country so he could grow up like she had. But that just wasn't in the cards for a single mother.

She slowed, closing her eyes briefly to let in all the sounds and smells she could. If she had her way, she would have picked up her home and moved it to someplace similar to this.

"What are you doing here?"

Her eyes flew open to find Zeke stopped in the middle of the trail, the hardness from previous interactions returning. Agatha wrapped her light jacket around herself tighter and nodded in the direction she'd come. "I only came out here to ask you if you'd like to join me for breakfast."

She wasn't certain, but in the early morning light, it almost looked like his expression had softened. That small change had her heart on edge, fluttering like this was a meeting between two lovers rather than two strangers who really had no business spending time together.

"You want me to join you for breakfast."

"That's what I said." She forced her voice louder, praying it would cover the fact that he unnerved her. "And if you'd like to join me for breakfast from this point forward, I'm turning it into a standing offer. I'll not have you out here cooking over a fire while you work on my house."

His lips twitched. "So it's not an invitation. It's a demand."

The fluttering went into hyperdrive, and her stomach tightened. "I won't force you to do anything, Mr. Callahan—"

He waved his hand at her. "Call me Zeke. You've used my name before. There's no need to be so formal."

It was as if her insides had decided to go on some thrilling fair ride where she didn't know if the contraption would even remain in operating condition. Her stomach went in one direction while her lungs went in another. Agatha had to force her eyes away from him in order to regain some semblance of composure.

Enough with the formalities? Was he suggesting that they were shifting into something more... *personal*?

Agatha turned away, biting back a smile. Her thoughts were in a whirlwind. She'd gone from distrusting him and not liking him to suddenly thinking he wasn't such a bad guy. It was possible he was exactly who he presented on the surface.

Were there things that rubbed her the wrong way? Sure. But there wasn't a single person who didn't have their flaws. She certainly did. Who was she to judge Zeke? There was no reason for it.

"You're going the wrong way."

Stopping, Agatha let her gaze sweep the immediate

surroundings. No, this was the trail she'd come from. There was no way she'd gotten turned around.

"I don't know how you got all the way out here, but I'm guessing you made a wrong turn," Zeke's gruff voice called out to her.

This time she turned to face him. "No, I'm certain I came from this direction."

"You keep heading that way and you're going to find yourself at a creek. It's beautiful, but I wouldn't go out that way this early in the morning. You're most certainly going to meet up with some animals that would consider you to be their breakfast."

She swallowed hard. "I thought you said there weren't any animal tracks around."

Zeke chuckled, a small smile appearing on his face—one of the first genuine ones he'd given her. "I didn't say the creek was close. It's a good half-hour walk in that direction. But I'm sure with your determination, you could make it there in half that time."

Another compliment? Or was he teasing? Based on his expression, she didn't have a single clue.

He nodded to her left. "That's the way you want to take." Without waiting for her, he trudged off in that direction. She followed behind him, glancing over her shoulder a couple times as if doing so would help her make sense of how she'd gotten so turned around.

It didn't help even one iota.

The second the cabin loomed in front of her, the disorientation seemed to right itself. She didn't know how she managed to get so off course, but at least Zeke had been in the right place at the right time. That seemed to be happening more and more lately.

Zeke strode right up to the front door, then waited. She stopped a few feet from him, confused. "Is something wrong?"

He gestured toward the door. "I don't live here."

The puzzle pieces in her mind still didn't connect. "But it's your cabin."

"Ms. Birch, I would never enter a woman's home even if I owned the property."

The initial surprise at his perspective faded as she focused on one thing. He didn't use her first name. She placed her hand on her hip and gave him a pointed look. "What happened to being less formal?"

His face crinkled as he tossed her a smile.

Agatha rolled her eyes, letting out an exaggerated sigh. A smile of her own crossed her face as she strode past him. She opened the door, then gestured in a sweeping motion. "Guests first."

Zeke removed his hat and headed inside.

The table was already set and the food sat warm on the stove, waiting for her return. She could sense Zeke's surprised look more than anything and focused on not meeting it as she brought the food to the table.

If she thought their encounter in the woods was bad, she wasn't prepared for the awkwardness of sharing their meal. He was quiet, and just like before, he continued to glance at her. It got to the point where she needed to just break through the glass of tension she could feel around them.

Agatha lifted her head, not at all surprised to find him staring at her. "What's happening today?"

Zeke wiped his mouth with his napkin and settled back in his seat. "Tuck said we should be getting the new flooring in today."

"Really? I thought we wouldn't install the flooring for at least a few more weeks."

He shook his head. "We won't be installing the flooring. We have to paint first. If we do it that way, then we run a smaller risk of ruining it. Then after paint and flooring, we'll get the cabinets installed. From there it's tiling, baseboards, and finishing the bathroom upstairs."

"Sounds like everything is falling into place. How much time do you think that will take? A month or two?"

Zeke shook his head, another soft laugh on his lips. "All of the framework and drywall got done fast because we had a lot of men on site. From this point forward, it's only going to be Tuck and me."

It was hard to fight the disappointment. That is until she realized she'd have an excuse to spend more time with Zeke. She stole another glance at him, wondering how the next several weeks would go if she were open to getting to know him more on his level. Now that he'd stopped bossing her around, he was actually a joy to visit with.

Agatha turned her focus to her food. "I hear Grace is expecting. She's the one who's married to Tristan, right?"

"It's Dianna who's expecting."

She ducked her head. "Sorry. I must have gotten them mixed up. I don't know how you did it all on your own—raising seven girls, I mean. That had to be incredibly difficult." Agatha half-expected him to play it off like most parents did. But she was wrong.

"It was hard." He said it simply. There was no smirk nor a hardened stare. Zeke was just matter-of-fact about the whole thing. "When you have seven girls and they don't have a mother figure to go to when things get…" He cleared his throat, the first sign of discomfort. "… rough. But I think we came out all right."

"Based on what I've seen, I'd say you're right." She said it softly, referring to the fine young men his daughters ended up with.

"Why do you say that?"

She shrugged. "I suppose it's clear to me that your daughters were raised to respect themselves and demand that same kind of respect from the men in their lives."

He considered her for a moment, then nodded before turning back to his food. "I would say the same about Thomas."

His compliment had been unexpected, but the reaction that started inside her was even more so. She smiled, unable to repress this one. It wasn't often that she was complimented for the way she'd raised her son. She'd always hoped that Thomas would turn out to be the kind of man that would make her proud but also a man who would show the world just how wonderful he could be. "Thank you," she murmured.

Zeke glanced at her, gave her a tight nod, then gathered his dishes and headed to the sink. "We should probably get going."

OVER THE NEXT FEW WEEKS, while they didn't speak much, Agatha felt she'd gotten a good feel for who Zeke was—the person behind all the gossip and soft-spoken words. He was a man of character. He was strong and sure of himself, but he cared for others in a way no one expected of him.

He was generous to a fault. Between what he'd done to help her get set up and what he'd done to help another nearby ranch, Agatha had a hard time trying to come up with things to hate about him.

The more time she spent with him, the more difficult it was to *not* find him utterly attractive. During the day she was plagued with the urge to ask him out on an official date. And at night she had to deal with dreams of those very events taking place.

It was getting to a point where she knew she needed to do something about it or it would drive her crazy.

On a Friday, they had to cut things short. The deliveries had been delayed due to some unforeseen situations and they simply ran out of work to do. The whole ride back to the cabin, as she clasped her hands tighter around his middle, she repeated the words in her head she wanted to say to him.

Asking a man out shouldn't be this difficult. They lived in the modern era. And Zeke seemed to have warmed up to her. He was friendlier, he smiled more, and he didn't seem to mind when she insisted on helping out at the house.

There were even a few moments when she thought he might say something, but then she thought better of it. Those were the moments when she could have sworn he was having the same kinds of feelings about her.

The ATV came to a stop, and she climbed off. This was her chance. They had an early day and she could ask him if he'd like to go get dinner. That simple.

But then Zeke started up the engine rather than climbing off the ATV. He gave her a nod, and the vehicle started moving forward.

Agatha didn't know what possessed her, but she darted out in front of it. Her hands landed hard on the front, and she blushed the moment he shot her a surprised and almost lethal look. Zeke shut off the engine and stood. "What in the name of..." He tore his hat from his head and clutched it tightly in one hand. "You could have got yourself hurt."

"Go out with me," she blurted. It wasn't even a question. It was a statement, and one that she really wished she hadn't practically shouted. She blushed again and looked away. "I mean, I would love it if you'd... if we... could go on a date."

He didn't speak right away. In fact, he waited so long that she was forced to lift her eyes to meet his. And she wished she hadn't done that either.

If the surprise on his face wasn't enough, she could have sworn she saw a flicker of guilt, or perhaps it was pity. Both looked the same right about now. "Agatha—"

Agatha held up her hands, stopping him from speaking.

"Just think about it, okay? And if the answer is no. I totally understand." Without waiting for a response, she rushed toward the cabin. That had to be the most embarrassing moment she'd had since she was a teenager.

But at least she'd done it. No regrets.

13

———

Zeke

It was all Zeke could do to keep himself from going after Agatha when she escaped into the cabin. There were so many things wrong with what had just happened. He sat frozen in his seat, swinging his gaze to the cabin, then back to the road in front of him.

He really should just go knock on her door and tell her that he was going on a date with another woman tonight. That would be the proper thing to do.

While it was a first date and there were no plans for it to go further than just tonight, he didn't want to make any assumptions. If he were to hit it off with this woman, then Agatha was bound to find out.

Zeke removed the hat on his head and ran a hand through his hair. As much as he was ready for this date, he couldn't ignore the fact that he wished it was with a different person—the very one who was in that cabin a few yards away.

He stood, the intention to tell her everything a driving force, but then thought better of it. Zeke settled back into his seat. What was wrong with him? He had always been so sure of himself. He'd always known what he wanted and where his life was headed.

The man he was today wasn't the man he wanted to be.

His face scrunched into a scowl and he leaned forward as he gave the vehicle some gas. This was the right thing to do. He'd been over it and over it in his head. Agatha wasn't the kind of woman he could see himself with long-term, mostly because they had a tendency to butt heads. Lately it had been good-natured, but to spend the rest of his life with her? No, that wasn't going to work.

The woman Brielle had sworn would be a good fit had better be exactly that because he needed to get his mind off Agatha once and for all.

ONCE OUT OF THE SHOWER, Zeke got dressed and ready for his date. He still had an hour before he'd need to pick her up, and those sixty minutes stretched out before him like a tightrope with no net beneath it.

Tonight, he'd take a step he had never seen himself taking. And if nothing came of it? Then his daughters couldn't say a thing about him getting back out in the world. Some people only meet their perfect match once.

Armed with this personal breakthrough, Zeke headed toward the kitchen to get himself a drink but was stopped by Brielle in the living room.

"Well, don't you look handsome." Brielle moved away from a small group that was visiting. Her husband didn't meet Zeke's gaze. Wade appeared to prefer staying out of Zeke's line of focus.

Shane and Eloise were also visiting, and Zeke couldn't help

but feel he was the topic of conversation. His eyes narrowed as he took in the conspirators. "And you four look guilty as could be."

Brielle laughed as she straightened his bolo tie. "You really ought to wear one of your fancier ties tonight."

"Those ties are for weddings and funerals. I'm not going out in public wearing something like that," he said.

She looked up at him with a smile that had always been able to melt his heart, even when she'd been a little girl. "I'm glad you're going out either way. I know you're going to have fun."

"Don't get your hopes up. I don't even know the woman."

"Charlotte is a lovely lady, and I bet you'll hit it off."

Shane coughed, choking on something before he got it under control.

Zeke shot a dark look toward his soon-to-be son-in-law. "You have something to say?"

He straightened, shaking his head, though his easy smile appeared all the same. "No, sir. I'm sure Brielle has found the perfect match for you."

Why did it feel like Shane wasn't being entirely honest with him? Zeke studied the man who coincidently had his finger in nearly everything in town. It had happened slowly at first, but now he was almost married to Zeke's daughter, ran the most profitable businesses, and even hired the woman Zeke couldn't get out of his mind.

It was a good thing Shane was a decent man, or Zeke might have been tempted to get rid of him in a way that looked like an accident.

Shane shifted beneath Zeke's scrutiny. "Is there something you needed to tell me, sir?"

"Dad," Eloise warned.

Zeke dragged his focus to his daughter. "What?"

"Everything okay?" Eloise reached for Shane's hand, giving her father a pointed look.

Zeke sighed. Ever since he'd relinquished control over his family's lives, he couldn't seem to get his footing. Every day presented a new challenge that wore him down. He was supposed to be the king of the castle, the man in charge, and now what? He was the one who got pushed around by his daughters and his neighbor. "I'm fine. Just waiting until I can leave to pick up Charlotte."

"And it's going to be great," Brielle insisted.

"You keep saying stuff like that, and when it doesn't come true, you'll be the one I blame."

She laughed again. "You just need to get out there again—find someone who makes you smile, someone you can't stop thinking about."

That sounded an awful lot like Agatha.

No, it didn't, his head seemed to argue. *She makes you mad. She's irritatingly stubborn and thinks she knows better. She pushes your buttons in ways no one ever has. Do you really want to be with someone like that?*

His head had a point. He just had to keep reminding himself of that. Evelyn had been perfect for him. She'd had a quiet strength that he could lean on, but she knew when to let him take the lead. No other woman he'd met in his life had the same kind of qualities, nor could they hold a candle to the woman he'd loved for over a decade.

Agatha was a near opposite of his late wife, and while he had grown to be friendly with her—perhaps even somewhat attracted to her—he knew when to pull himself back to reality.

Zeke pulled away from Brielle and let his gaze sweep through the room again until it landed on Shane. The young man seemed to grow incredibly still. It was as if he knew instinctively that Zeke was going to request to speak to him alone before it even happened.

Shane got to his feet at the same moment Zeke cleared his throat. "Shane, a word?"

Eloise was the only one who looked even a little surprised by the request. Thankfully, Brielle and Wade didn't seem to notice anything amiss.

Zeke jerked his chin toward the front door, then strode in that direction, knowing Shane would follow him.

They stepped out onto the front porch, and Shane closed the door behind him. Zeke rested his folded arms on the porch railing and squinted. "The rodeo is just about over."

Shane didn't respond, though his shuffling made it clear he was still present.

"Agatha has been looking into a few motels that might have room after all the tourists and cowboys leave."

"That's news to me."

Zeke cocked a brow at Shane over his shoulder. "When this whole fiasco began, she was insistent she wouldn't stay in my cabin. But when she found out about the availability around here, she changed her tune."

"Okay, I'm admit, I'm curious as to why you're bringing this up to me."

"Have you seen the state of the motel in town? It can barely be classified as a hole in the wall. I was wondering if you heard anything about her looking for other accommodations."

Shane rubbed his jaw as he moved closer. He leaned his back against the railing on the other side of the stairs, his arms folded. "She hasn't mentioned anything to me. Though, to be honest, she's usually kept her personal life to herself. Agatha values being professional above all else. I don't even think she would request help if she thought I could offer it. In fact, I'm surprised she accepted the help you gave her. I can only imagine the fight she put up."

A smile tugged at Zeke's lips. "I didn't really give her much of a choice."

"No, I didn't suppose you did."

They stood there quietly as Zeke retreated into his own thoughts. He probably shouldn't have even brought up Agatha with Shane. He clearly wasn't going to get what he needed from the man.

"May I ask why you asked?" Shane said.

Zeke pressed his lips together tightly. He didn't dare show his cards. If Shane even got a whiff that Zeke was attracted to Agatha, he had no doubt the man would spill his guts to those seated in the living room. "I was hoping you'd be a voice of reason, but from the sounds of it, she won't listen to you any more than she'd listen to me."

Shane chuckled. "You'd be right about that. But you know who she might listen to?"

Zeke gave him a blank stare.

"Her son. Thomas works for you, doesn't he?"

All he could muster was a grunt. Pulling Tom aside and telling him to speak to Agatha on his account sounded even worse than speaking with Shane. At least Shane had the smarts to be discreet. Who knew what Tom might assume?

Zeke pulled away from the railing. "I'll give it some thought. It might not even be an issue. I think she's grown accustomed to having her own little retreat out in the wooded area."

"That wouldn't surprise me." Shane smiled. "Oh, and since we're discussing Agatha's rebuild, I wanted to offer some funding—anonymously of course."

"Of course."

Shane held out his hand for Zeke to shake, and he accepted. "Thanks, Mr. Callahan."

Zeke clapped him on the shoulder. "You're family now. No need to be so formal."

Another chuckle reverberated from his chest. "Perhaps in time. You're still just as intimidating as the day I heard about you." Shane headed inside, and Zeke lingered on the porch.

Funny how quickly Zeke had grown accustomed to Agatha's presence in the cabin and how tempted he was to call the motel and buy up all the rooms to prevent her from leaving.

He wouldn't do that. But the thought still lingered in the back of his mind.

~

ZEKE FINGERED the fancy fabric napkin at Shane's restaurant. This was the first time he'd stayed at the country club for more than a few minutes and the only time he'd come to the restaurant.

From what he could tell, it stood up to the hype. Shane had done very well for himself. It wasn't any wonder why Eloise loved working in the kitchen as well.

Charlotte's voice echoed around him, and he glanced up to find her chatting away. She was soft-spoken but still a chatterbox, reminding him of the songbirds that woke him in the early morning hours.

Petite, with a small, upturned nose and dyed black hair, she could have been compared to a field mouse. Zeke was beginning to realize why Brielle had thought they'd hit it off. This woman, while not physically similar to his late wife, had some mannerisms like her. Evelyn didn't talk nearly as much, but she blushed easily, and her laugh was infectious.

Charlotte was similar in those ways. She looked away, her cheeks burning. "I'm sorry. There I go rambling on again without giving you a chance to say two words. Tell me something about yourself. Your daughter mentioned that you have a profitable ranch and that your late wife passed when she was a little girl, but I'm afraid I don't know much else."

Why was it that when Zeke gazed at this woman, he found himself wanting to be with someone else—someone who wasn't afraid to meet his eyes for longer than a few seconds?

"Zeke?"

He jumped, and her face came into focus.

"Are you okay?"

"Yes, my apologies. I'm a bit distracted."

"Oh? Is there something wrong?"

Zeke shook his head. "Not anymore. My neighbor—her house burned down a little over two months ago and I'm working with some of my men to get it rebuilt."

Charlotte gasped. "Oh, gracious. I hope everyone got out okay."

He nodded. "Yes, it's mostly just property damage. We're getting closer to finishing the basic stuff, and then we'll move on to the more designer aspects."

She reached across the table and touched his hand but pulled away just as quickly. "That's so wonderful—you helping her, that is. I don't know of many who would offer." Her eyes dropped to her lap. "She must mean a lot to you."

Zeke gave her a funny look—one she missed due to her intense focus on her hands that were now in her lap. "Why would you say that?"

Charlotte's eyes flitted up to meet his and she smiled. "Just like I said. It's not often that someone would help their neighbor just out of the goodness of their heart."

"Well, my mother raised me right. I'm just going to assume you're referring to the men of this generation."

"You may be right," Charlotte said. "Regardless, I think it's very kind and generous."

He nearly thanked her, but that wasn't why he was helping Agatha. He didn't need recognition or praise. He was doing it because... well, because it needed to be done and he had the means to do it.

Zeke gave a sharp nod of his head as if he'd won an argument with himself.

Charlotte's smile widened. "I've had a wonderful time with

you tonight, and I just wanted to assure you that while I'd love a second date, I get the strangest feeling that your heart might be elsewhere."

Confusion clouded his thoughts. "My heart? My heart isn't *anywhere*. I wasn't even sure I wanted to go on a date in the first place. I'd love to see you again if that's what you're getting at."

"Honey," her voice was irritatingly patronizing, "you might think you're not ready to date, but I would wager you're far more prepared than you realize. But you have to find that person that has a... *spark*." She got to her feet. "This was lovely. I enjoyed the food and the company, but I believe you're better suited for someone else."

It was hard not to be offended by her statement. He scrambled to his feet as she strode toward the exit. Zeke shrugged into his jacket and threw down some bills for the tip, then hurried after her.

By the time he caught up with her, she was taking the stairs, only that wasn't the thing that threw him off balance.

At the base of the stairs stood the one person he didn't want to see.

14

Agatha

gatha couldn't believe her eyes. Staring at her from the top of the steps at her place of work was none other than Zeke Callahan. And from the looks of it, he was chasing after his own Cinderella.

Shoot, shoot, shoot, shoot!

If she thought asking him out was bad, seeing him with another woman was ten times worse.

Of course he was dating someone.

This man—a cowboy who apparently had a heart of gold— also had a woman to hold when his nights were lonely and cold.

Agatha's stomach turned to stone, weighing her down and rooting her to the spot. Her eyes darted from the pretty woman to the cowboy she'd grown attached to.

Jealousy writhed within her, and she abhorred the sensation even as her face flushed hotter than the sun itself. If she'd been smart, she would have waited around long enough earlier today to let Zeke get a word in edgewise rather than running off and forcing him to have to deal with it all.

She wanted to groan, to stomp her foot and race off toward the restroom—anything to stop her from feeling so mortified.

The woman glanced over her shoulder toward Zeke, then back to Agatha. She smiled sweetly. "Hello, I'm Charlotte. I take it you know Zeke?"

Great. Just great.

This Charlotte woman knew him by his first name. They were *familiar*. Well, duh. They were dressed up and leaving the country club together on a Friday evening.

Agatha's face burned hotter, though she didn't think it was possible. Even her mouth seemed to simmer. "Yes, we're uh... he's..." She bounced one fist against her thigh. She could look away, show her submission, make herself miserable, or she could shove her pain back at Zeke and let him take some of it. He was partly to blame for all of this. Agatha crossed her arms and put all her weight onto one foot. She forced the biggest smile she could muster. "We're neighbors."

Charlotte's eyes widened and she looked once more toward Zeke. "You must be the woman he's helping out. I'm so sorry to hear about the fire."

She didn't know whether to feel elated or horrified that she'd been the topic of conversation between these two. Clearly, Charlotte didn't feel the least bit threatened by her, so it was probably the latter. "Thank you," she murmured. Telling this woman that she hadn't heard anything about her clung to the tip of her tongue, but Agatha was better than that. She didn't need to bring down another person simply because something didn't work out for her.

No. She'd be the bigger person, and Zeke could find his happily ever after with someone else. Agatha would be fine—as soon as she managed to lick her wounds and hide away from the world for a day or so. Strange how this embarrassment hit harder than she had expected. She hadn't stepped foot inside a high school for decades, and yet this ache seemed to burn just as it would have in her teen years.

Agatha smiled at Charlotte, then forced herself to meet Zeke's eyes. "I'm just here to pick up some paperwork from Shane's office and I'll be on my way. Sorry to interrupt your evening." She hurried up the steps, but her toe snagged on one and down, down, down, she fell until a hand shot out and stopped her from face-planting entirely.

It happened all so fast. Zeke had managed to grab ahold of her in such a way that she only suffered a bruise to the shin.

While her lower leg throbbed excruciatingly, her heart did the same but more deliciously. She stared into Zeke's eyes, and for the briefest of moments, she could almost see what a future with him might have been like.

His face was so close. The warmth from his body emanated just far enough to graze her chilled skin. All of the kind things he'd said to her up until this moment made it that much harder for her to come to her senses and pull away.

"Thanks," she rasped. "You saved me... again. I'm sure you're getting tired of it."

"Never," he whispered under his breath.

Her eyes cut to meet his, uncertain if she'd heard him actually say that single word or if it was all in her imagination. But when their gazes locked, she knew deep down she'd lost it. She put more distance between them and waved toward Charlotte. "It was nice to meet you. I hope you two enjoy your evening together."

Agatha couldn't escape into the building fast enough. Not even the music or loud chatter could scrape all the goosebumps from her flesh. She rubbed her arms vigorously. How was she supposed to face him tomorrow when he stopped by for breakfast?

What had she done!

That standing invitation wasn't supposed to come back to bite her. She'd merely wanted to offer him something to show her appreciation. And now she'd gummed everything up.

NEVER IN HER wildest dreams did Agatha think that anything could get any worse than it already had.

She'd lost her home, her memories, her property.

Now, she'd lost her dignity and grace.

Technically, Zeke was never hers to begin with, but somehow she felt like she'd lost a future with him, which didn't make any more sense the more time that passed between the moment at the country club and where she now sat on the cabin steps.

Zeke wasn't back yet, and if he was, it was far more likely he was avoiding her than anything else. Only she had a major problem.

She'd locked herself out of the cabin.

Already, she'd checked all the windows. She'd checked all the doors and even the places where he might have hidden a hide-a-key.

There was no salvation.

Agatha dug her hands into her hair again and again, completely messing it up beyond repair. She wasn't even sure a brush would be able to tame her disheveled tresses. Finding a new place to live was beginning to sound better and better with each passing second.

She wouldn't even mind staying in her home now that the exterior was done. The paint fumes weren't all that terrible.

Zeke wouldn't go for it, but what control did he have over her?

None.

Zilch.

Now, if he didn't have a girlfriend and they'd followed through with their date, perhaps she'd give him a vote.

Okay, probably not even then, but at least she wouldn't be drumming up ideas of how to avoid the man. When had she turned into a coward? This wasn't who she was. She wasn't helpless, nor did she care what other people thought of her.

But Zeke wasn't just some random person. Somewhere along the line, she'd grown affectionate toward him. And that was where the problem resided.

"Agatha?"

She jumped, her eyes narrowing as she stared into the darkness surrounding the cabin. She would have recognized that voice anywhere, and already the adrenaline had kicked in, preparing her fight or flight instinct.

Agatha got to her feet and curled her hand around the railing. "Zeke."

He stepped into the light that spilled from the porch awning. Still dressed in his slacks, button-up shirt, and bolo tie, he looked just as good as he did at the club—except his features were strained.

"What are you doing here, Zeke?" It was impossible to hide the accusation from her voice. "Shouldn't you be with Charlotte?"

Even from her vantage point, she could see the way his jaw tightened.

Agatha pressed forward, hating the silence even more than the betrayal she felt coiling in her stomach—betrayal she wasn't even entitled to. "You shouldn't be here. If I had known you were dating someone..."

"I'm not," he ground out.

She let out a laugh that even startled herself. "You could have fooled me. Look, I don't care, all right? You don't owe me any explanations. We never went on a date or even... kissed." Shoot! Why did she have to bring that up? What was she thinking! Agatha sucked in a deep breath, closed her eyes, then opened them again. "It's good—you dating. I don't know why it surprised me. But it's fine."

His left eye twitched. "Charlotte isn't my girlfriend, and we're certainly not *dating*."

"I've been down this road before. I don't need your life story or what this woman may or may not mean to you. I just need a key so I can get back inside."

Zeke's expression faltered as his focus shifted to the cabin. "The key?"

"Yeah. I need your spare. I forgot that I didn't have mine when I locked up."

He sighed as he pulled out a keyring from his pocket. Trudging up the steps, Zeke fiddled with the ring until he found the key he was looking for and then he shoved it into the door.

The knob clicked. He retrieved his key. Then he turned to face her. "About earlier."

She waved her hand dismissively. "Don't even worry about it. I took a chance, and it didn't pan out. Honestly, I should have known better." She brushed past him to get inside, but she wasn't fast enough.

His hand grasped onto hers, tugging her away from the door. "What is that supposed to mean?"

"You know..."

Zeke's brows pulled together, creasing between them. "You're going to have to enlighten me."

It took a great deal more strength than she realized to be able to say what she wanted to say next. Agatha pulled free of him and met him square in the eyes. "You should probably leave now. Whether or not you've labeled it as a relationship, it's clear something is going on between you and Charlotte. I'm not going to come between that."

Her hand tightened around the doorknob, and she pushed

it open. As quickly as she could, she shut the door, but it stopped with a thud. A boot protruded into her safe haven, and she peered out the crack in the open doorway. "Kindly remove your boot from the door so I can shut it."

"For the last time, I'm not with Charlotte."

She rolled her eyes. "I'm not some delicate flower—"

"And I pity the fool who doesn't have the brains to realize you are the furthest thing from a flower there is."

Her head snapped back. "I beg your pardon."

He nudged the door open a little farther as he inched closer. "You're not delicate, Agatha."

She didn't know whether to be offended by that statement or simply curious.

Again, he got closer, pushing the door open enough that she had to step backward. Her heart fluttered wildly, not out of fear but something else entirely. Agatha sidestepped as he entered the cabin and somehow found herself against the closed door with Zeke hovering a few feet away.

"Do you have any idea how hard it is to go on a date with someone when all you can think about is someone else?" His voice was low, husky, like the purr of a large mountain cat.

The hairs on the back of her neck stood on end, and her fingers sought for purchase on the smooth wood door. Throat painfully dry, Agatha simply stared up at the man who had managed to get her full attention.

His hand pressed firmly against the door right above her shoulder as he trapped her with his fiery gaze. "Do you understand how painful it is to know that to act on certain feelings would spell assured disaster, and the only way to steer clear is to avoid that person at all costs?"

She blinked rapidly. This was not where she thought this conversation was going.

Logic and irrationality battled so deftly that she couldn't gauge which one was more correct. Zeke couldn't possibly be talking about her. He'd been nicer lately, which was probably why she'd suddenly found herself so much more attracted to him.

Zeke cupped her chin, his eyes scanning her face as if he were able to drink her in. "You want to know what I was thinking when you showed up at that club?"

"No," she whispered.

That seemed to give him pause. Ironically, she'd uttered the word without realizing she'd said it out loud. Agatha swallowed hard and pulled her head away enough that she was no longer staring into his eyes. "You made me feel like a fool today, Zeke. I still feel a little hungover from meeting a woman who was clearly nothing like me. If you have a type—"

"You're nothing like my type, Agatha."

She shot him a sharp look, her irritation returning, fueling her sense of self-worth. "Then what are we even talking about?" She moved to duck beneath his arm, but he stopped her.

"I wish I could explain it. Really I do. I wish I knew what was going on, because I haven't ever felt this way about a woman." He shook his head, his eyes getting a far-off look in them. "The whole drive home, I've come to realize one thing."

"What's that?"

His eyes finally locked with hers. "It doesn't matter."

"Of course it does," she blurted. "You can't stand there and tell me that thinking about me brings you pain, or that you want to avoid me, that I'm not your type and that none of it matters! Do you even hear yourself? You sound crazy. Of course it matters," she repeated. "All of that matters whether you like it or not. People don't simply get together because something in their gut tells them to. There has to be attraction and—"

Without any warning, his lips dropped over hers, gentle and explorative. The lightest brush of warmth against her cool skin sent a shiver down her spine. His hand reached around the back of her neck, caressing her skin.

Agatha's lashes fluttered closed, and her heart thundered in time with the hooves of the wild horses she'd seen on occasion. Slowly, her arms slipped around Zeke and she rose on her toes.

Closer, she needed to be enveloped by him—taking every part of his soul into her own. The connection between them was more than merely electric; it was like a wildfire that had gone rogue.

Dangerous—that's what this was.

And it was deliciously consuming her to her very core.

15

———

*H*olding Agatha this way stirred up some feelings that had long since been buried. Zeke lost himself with her in his arms. She sparked something inside him that remained just out of reach—unable to be scrutinized just yet.

He could go on kissing her like this until the sun came up, but that wasn't written in his stars. Agatha's hands pressed gently against his chest, pushing him back a step. He blinked, his vision blurry as she came into focus.

Normally, he might feel a degree of shame for what he'd done. He'd assumed that she wanted the kiss as much as he did. Hadn't she mentioned earlier that they hadn't even kissed yet? But if any man would have done the same to his daughters, he would have drilled them into the ground with his bare hands.

Only, this felt different. It was like he'd finally connected with what he needed. It wasn't just a relationship. It was Agatha.

She wasn't meeting his gaze as she continued to lean up against the door. Her nose and cheeks had turned a soft pink color like a gentle sunrise. He itched to reach out and caress her, tell her everything he was feeling in this very moment.

But something held him back.

It was probably due to the way she'd put that space between them. She wasn't ready. How was it that they couldn't get their timing right? "Agatha?" he whispered.

She shifted, though she wouldn't meet his eyes.

"I need you to talk to me." His heart thundered. There was no way she didn't hear it beating against his chest like a raging storm.

"Why did you do that?" she said.

"Why did I do what?"

When she set her focus on him, his blood heated. The intensity behind her gaze had him reeling. "Why did you kiss me like that?"

"You're not serious," he murmured, reaching for her on instinct.

Agatha waved off his hand and shook her head. "You just came from a date with another woman. What am I supposed to believe?"

"Is that what this is about?" Zeke let out a dry chuckle. "My daughter set me up with Charlotte. Tonight was the first time I'd even met the woman."

Agatha didn't look convinced.

He ran a hand down his face and forced himself to remain cool and collected. It wouldn't help his case if he lost his temper. "Charlotte is a lovely lady, but even she said that I wasn't supposed to be on that date with her." Their conversation at her doorstep had been one of the most awkward ones he'd experienced in his lifetime. She refused to hug him, and there were no kisses exchanged. "All she permitted was a handshake when I dropped her off."

Her eyes narrowed. "Sounds like you expected more."

"*What*? No. Of course not." The heat crawled up the back of his neck and flooded his face. "It was a first date. I don't expect that sort of thing from women on the first date."

Agatha's lips twitched at the corners. "No, you just corner them and kiss them without warning."

Zeke gaped at her. She'd caught him in a tough spot, and she knew it. What could he say to that? There was nothing. He couldn't argue with her, nor could he make excuses. "My apologies," he finally said. Zeke stepped back another few feet. "I've overstepped."

"Yes, you have."

He waited for her to open the door, to shoo him out of her home and let him run with his tail between his legs, but she didn't move. Instead, she studied him, her head tilted, her eyes still bright. "You really only just met her?"

Zeke stiffened. What possible reason would she have to ask such a thing? "I wouldn't lie to you, Agatha. Certainly not about that."

"And what you said about... that you couldn't stop thinking about me..."

"All of it was true."

She shook her head. "This isn't a good idea."

"Why not?" he blurted. "You were the one who asked me out."

"Yes, I did. And I was wrong to do so."

Zeke spun around, taking a few steps away from her as he ran his hand through his hair. "I'm sorry, Agatha, but you're going to have to explain a little more than that."

"It wasn't until I saw you at the country club with Charlotte that the truth really settled with me. It's not just the fact that

people around here stick their noses where they don't belong—
though that's a pretty big reason."

"That shouldn't matter."

"You're right. It shouldn't. But it does. Because I don't want
my relationship to be public knowledge. Not with you—not
with anyone."

Zeke let out a sigh. He could understand where she was
coming from, but something about her words didn't match up
with what he knew of her. "I thought you didn't care what other
people thought."

"I don't," she insisted. "But I'll not have my love life gossiped
about when it comes to my son. You're his boss. How do you
think that would look? His mother dating the man who pays
his bills?"

He stilled. Everything inside him wanted to brush her off, to
remind her that Thomas was an adult and he could handle any
kind of gossip that made the rounds. But it wasn't just Thomas's
feelings that mattered. Based on how his daughters had reacted
when he was getting ready for his date, he could tell they had
their hopes up as well.

Agatha wasn't the kind of woman he would have ever
picked out for himself. The way he was so irrevocably drawn to
her even made him nervous.

"See? You know I'm telling the truth. Besides Thomas and
the folks in town, I just don't see a way that we'd be able to
work it out—especially considering your personality."

Zeke straightened to his full height and set stern eyes on
her. "What about my personality?"

Her smile was tentative this time. "It's not a *bad* thing. You're
just... controlling."

"*Controlling?*"

"Well, yeah. Everything is your way or the highway. That's
how it's been since the moment we met."

"Me? What about you? You're the most irritatingly stubborn

woman I have ever met. I'd say you'd give a mule a run for his money, but you're so far out of his league you'd make a mockery of him."

Her smile faded, and her lips pressed into a tight line. "You just can't seem to get your head around the fact that I'm my own person. I've lived my life raising my son without any help from anyone. I didn't need it then, and I don't need it now."

"Everyone needs help—even you. Without me, your house wouldn't be getting rebuilt for another year, probably."

"And if I didn't put my foot down on certain aspects of that rebuild, then you'd end up behind schedule. Or have you forgotten about the time your men were going to start drywalling the upstairs without the proper insulation?"

They stared at each other, neither wavering, for what felt like an eternity. Then Zeke released a pent-up breath. "Fine. We're both too stubborn for our own good."

"Exactly. I don't know what I was even thinking when I asked you out on a date. It would never work." Agatha dropped her hands to her sides and shook her head. "I should have just kept my mouth shut."

All he could think about was the way her lips felt, the way her body pressed against his. In this moment his disappointment was enough to make him nauseated. He peeked at her, then down at his hands as he curled them into fists and released them. "This might just be something out of our control."

"Yeah... wait, what?"

"I'd be lying if I said I was willing to walk away."

"What are you saying?" Her voice sounded dry, and it broke on the last word.

"I'm saying that I'd be willing to give this a try if you are. Any parameters you want to set out, I'll follow them." Zeke moved closer to her but didn't reach out to touch her just yet.

"It might be a stupid risk—us trying out whatever this is that's grown between us. But I think it's worth it."

"You want us to start seeing each other?"

"Is that so hard to believe?" This time he grazed her jawline with his thumb. "I've never met anyone like you, and even though everything inside me is telling me to run, I... can't. I'd much rather risk it all than never know what could have been."

Agatha didn't move a muscle. She stared at him with wide eyes. "You can't possibly be serious."

"Oh, I'm serious. I can't ignore the fact that over the last several weeks, you are the one I can't stop thinking about. Is it possible that we won't work out? Certainly. But wouldn't it be fun to go along for the ride and see what happens?"

She lifted a single brow. "I thought you valued being in control. What you're suggesting goes against everything you say you need."

"I'm not getting any younger. What do I have to lose?" The words tumbled from his lips before he had a chance to really think about them. Agatha had made several good points, and if he'd gotten a good night's sleep and addressed this issue in the morning, he might have been a little more level-headed. Right now, all he could think about was kissing her again. Zeke shifted closer, dipping his face toward her.

But Agatha pushed against his chest with two of her fingers. "It's tempting."

His lips curled into a small smile. "Come on, Agatha. Take a chance, have some fun."

She sucked in a deep breath, her eyes never leaving his. "Okay, but we're going to lay out all the ground rules like you said."

"And what might those be?" His voice lowered and he glanced down at her lips. One more kiss. He'd do whatever it took to be wrapped up in her embrace just once more.

Agatha placed her hand against his cheek, and he leaned into her touch. "I know this sounds strange, but I really do think we need to keep whatever this is under wraps. I don't want Thomas to find out before I'm ready to tell him, and if anyone catches us together, it would only be a matter of time."

"You really think he'd mind?"

She pressed her lips together firmly. He could see the battle of wills behind her eyes. He'd experienced this side of that very look several times. There was a good chance she wouldn't be willing to share any information regarding her son with him, and he'd have to be okay with that. Agatha let out a sigh and dropped her hand to her side. "You have to understand that for the vast majority of his life, it has only ever been just the two of us. I can't even recall a time when he was interested in a woman for himself. We've always only looked out for each other. It's one of the big reasons I moved out here with him."

The look on Zeke's face must have told it all because she held up both hands and waved them. "I don't want you to get the wrong idea. It's not that he can't handle being on his own. I believe this is his way of paying me back for all of the years I spent raising him. He wants to make sure I'm taken care of and..." Agatha shrugged. She glanced up at him, then tore her gaze away from him just as quickly. "You must think this is terrible."

"On the contrary."

She stiffened, her gaze cutting to meet his.

Zeke chuckled. "I'm very well versed in this sort of dependency. Have you forgotten so easily that once upon a time, I treated my daughters in a way that prevented them from going out on their own? I can empathize with the young man. But there will come a day when he will need to branch out and find a lovely young woman to care for."

No words. Agatha seemed to be staring at him in shock. He couldn't tell if it was due to his being understanding or if she read some kind of condescending tone in his voice. He wasn't trying to sound superior. It just so happened that he'd had to learn the hard way that his daughters needed to get out on their own.

He cleared his throat and glanced away. "What I'm trying to say is that I'm not quite ready for my daughters to find out either. If you're concerned about Thomas, and I'm concerned about the girls, then I think we can safely say we're on the same page. We don't have to share what's developing between us with anyone until we're ready."

"Are you sure? Do you even think it's… possible?"

She made a good point. He hadn't considered how hard it would be to engage in a relationship without the folks around town noticing. "I don't know."

Agatha frowned. "If you don't think—"

"I said I didn't know. There will always be a learning curve when something changes in your life. How many people have to deal with this sort of thing all the time? I'd wager famous people have to keep their relationships quiet. Why can't we do the same? We can spend time together outside of the public eye. It shouldn't be that hard."

"Perhaps you're right." And just like that, the smile returned to her face. "It's not like we haven't been spending our fair share in each other's company as of late. We simply have to be aware of how we treat each other when anyone else is around."

He nodded. "Right."

A soft sound nearly resembling a giggle burst from her lips. "I can't believe I'm actually agreeing to this."

Zeke took both of her hands in his. "I can."

"That's not fair. You don't even know me."

"I know you're strong, independent, and a pain in the you-know-what when you want to get your way."

She laughed. "Sure doesn't sound like the kind of woman you'd want in your life."

He tugged her closer. "You are definitely not the kind of woman I would have considered even five years ago. But perhaps that's part of the fun. This… what's happening between us… it's exciting."

"I couldn't agree more."

16

———

Agatha

gatha pointed at the wall where Riley needed to add a bit more texture. "Right there. If we paint over that area, it will definitely be noticeable."

"With all due respect, ma'am. I've gone over that area at least three times."

"Well, you haven't done a good enough job at it." Agatha placed a hand on her hip. "The reason I'm here is to point out the small details that get overlooked." A pang of embarrassment and uncertainty swirled within her, and she nearly backed down. She had to remind herself that while a lot of these men were volunteers, she was allowed to ask them to touch up certain areas. If it didn't get fixed now, it would be a bigger headache later.

She could go track down Zeke and get his assistance on this matter, but she couldn't help wondering if doing so would draw too much attention to the two of them. Over the past couple of days, she'd put forth a lot of effort to keep her distance from the man whenever anyone was around.

Now, she stood up against one of Zeke's sons-in-law trying to explain why this was so important without stepping on his toes. Her eyes drifted toward the spot where she could clearly see the texture was uneven, her will dissolving with each passing second.

"Come on, Riley. Even if you can't see the difference, she can. Just do it again." Wade moved past her, lugging a cardboard box containing the new tile for her bathroom. He didn't even bother meeting her gaze as he strode toward the stairs.

Riley sighed. "Where did you want me to focus?"

Agatha pointed again, relieved she didn't have to find Zeke this time. She didn't know how much longer she'd be able to boss these men around without any official pull, but for now, she could breathe easy.

They spent the next ten minutes painstakingly getting the wall exactly how she wanted it. Then she felt it.

Like a cool breeze on a warm day, she could feel his gaze on her.

Zeke.

She shivered, then rubbed her arms up and down vigorously. It took every ounce of her self-control not to turn to find his gaze. This was how it had been for the last several days. And as soon as they were done working here, he'd take her back to the cabin where they could spend some time just being themselves.

Another chill coursed down her spine.

"Ma'am?"

Agatha jumped and stared at Riley. "I'm sorry?"

"Is there anything else you've noticed that needs to be fixed? This texture stuff is almost gone, so you might want to choose wisely." While his tone was indifferent or perhaps a little irritated, at least his expression was kind. He was being so patient with her; she really should do something in return.

The whole wall actually looked better now that the one spot had been filled in. She took a step backward and appraised it much like she would any project she was working on for herself or anyone else for that matter.

Shaking her head, she offered Riley a smile. "I think it looks great. In a few hours we should be able to paint it." She touched his forearm, preventing him from moving on to the next project. "Thank you so much for humoring an old woman like myself."

Riley snorted. "If you're old, then I'm a cowboy."

"Is that supposed to make me feel better? I thought it was customary to deny a woman's comment regarding her age."

His laugh was the furthest thing from what she'd expected. "Oh, I'm sorry. I forget you're a transplant here like me. I'm a vet, not a real cowboy."

"I'm sorry, I fail to see how caring for animals precludes you from being considered a cowboy."

Riley shook his head. "You misunderstand. I served in the military."

She blushed white hot. Right. That's why he was so much more familiar than the rest of the young men. Riley was someone she'd seen a lot of at the country club. "I'm so sorry. I've seen you around the country club, too, right?" She'd been so distracted with the build of her home and Zeke that she hadn't taken time to really get to know the men, other than Shane, who came and went from the site.

"That wouldn't surprise me. I'm one of the group therapy leaders." Riley put down the bucket he'd been using to hold the drywall texture.

Her blush burned even hotter. He *worked* for Shane like she did. Now she really felt sheepish. She could brush off her humiliation and blame it on the fact that she didn't work with the therapists or anyone besides Shane, for that matter, but that wasn't who she was. Part of the reason she liked working for Shane was that he allowed her to take any approach to how she did her job. And she'd dropped the ball when it came to meeting his staff.

When this whole house fiasco was dealt with, she would be sure to make more of an effort when it came to those working at the country club.

Agatha turned back to the conversation they'd been having. "Well, if it makes any difference, I think you are just as much a cowboy as anyone else around here. My son was a transplant too. He grew up in the city, and when he said he wanted to come out here to the middle of nowhere and work, he did. Being a cowboy isn't what you do. It's the way you live your life. If you ask me, a cowboy is a man with integrity who takes care of those he loves." She gave him a small smile, hoping it would cover up her embarrassment. "And it doesn't hurt to know a thing or two about horses."

"You've got a lot to learn about the cowboys around here, ma'am." Riley chuckled. "But I appreciate the sentiment. Men like Zeke Callahan and Tuck are the backbone of places like this. It's not just how they live their lives or how they take care of their families. It's how they care for the whole community even when they have better things to do with their time and money. You will never find folks like them in any other place." He touched the brim of his hat and gave her a nod. "I'm going to do a once-over through the rest of the house, and then I need to get back to the club for my shift."

Riley's words weighed on her, not uncomfortably so, more like they grounded her somehow. He was a transplant too. He'd likely heard all there was about the strict cowboys that lived in this area—especially Zeke. There wasn't anything more complimentary that he could have said about the man who remained such a quiet force to be reckoned with.

These thoughts and more were all that consumed her mind as she moved from one room to the next, seeing but not *really* seeing the things that had been completed and had yet to be started.

If there was one thing she had learned in the last week or so, it was that there was more than met the eye when it came to Zeke Callahan.

And he wanted to be with her.

Agatha's insides fluttered wildly, making her feel like a young woman again. Since that evening when Zeke had come by to tell her he was interested in her, they'd been very cautious about who might see them together. Zeke would eat breakfast with her and take her to the site like they'd been doing since the beginning, but he had dinner with his family much like she did with Thomas. The few moments they'd managed to steal away to be with each other didn't seem like nearly enough. She wanted to continue to get to know him the way everyone else seemed to.

Before she had a chance to realize what was happening, a hand shot out from the laundry room and pulled her into the darkness. She gasped, her eyes finding Zeke in the dim lighting as he moved her just enough to the side to shut the door.

Darkness consumed them, and it took a bit for her eyes to adjust. Zeke's low voice was the only thing that made her feel like she wasn't floating in the utter darkness where they were—that and the thin streak of light coming from beneath the door at their feet. "I couldn't wait a single second more before I could do this." Zeke gently placed his finger beneath her chin and tilted her face toward him.

He brushed a whisper of a kiss against her lips, and the rest of her body reacted in kind. Warmth spread to all her extremities as she leaned into his touch.

Agatha released a soft sound of pleasure, a smile gracing her lips. "And here I was thinking you were avoiding me."

"Never," he whispered before bestowing another kiss to her lips. "We need to get out of here."

She laughed. "Now? There's too much work to do. Besides, I think everyone would notice if we left together and didn't come back."

"No. I need to take you out on a proper date."

"But we can't be seen—"

"Not in town. But I'm taking you out of that cabin and we're going to spend the evening together."

She blinked, barely able to make out his features. "But what about Thomas?"

"I'm sure you can come up with an excuse. Tell him that one of my daughters is going to take you to town to pick out some new tile for the bathroom. That shouldn't be too hard to sell, should it?" His warm whispers slipped around her, drawing her in and making her feel lighter somehow.

"You want to take me on a date?" she whispered, her thoughts hazy.

"I want to take you on a date." His fingers grazed her neck as he tucked a loose strand of hair behind her ear, setting off thousands of new goosebumps.

All the things that held her back from starting a relationship with anyone over the years were easily shoved to the back of her mind. She'd been through so much over the last few months that she deserved to find some happiness for herself. "Okay," she murmured. "Where are we going to go?"

"You let me worry about that." He kissed her quickly, then pulled back. "Just make sure your excuse is believable, and I'll pick you up at six." Zeke nudged her to the side and then pulled open the door.

She winced as the bright light covered him from head to toe, but that initial sting quickly dissipated when his smile came into view. His eyes crinkled at the corners, and they seemed to shine more than usual.

It was probably the sunlight reflected there, but she could pretend the brighter look was due to the way he felt about her.

Zeke disappeared from her view and she leaned against the washing machine, her hand to her chest. Whether it was the sneaking around or the endorphins released from starting a new relationship, it didn't matter. Right now, she felt seen.

Pulling her lips between her teeth, she nibbled on them, if only to prevent herself from smiling like a crazy person.

Footsteps approached, and she hurriedly pulled away from the washer to open a cupboard that hung above it.

"Mom? There you are. I've been looking for… you." Thomas glanced around the laundry room. "What are you doing in the dark?"

She glanced over her shoulder at him as nonchalantly as possible. "The men were working on something electrical and they shut off the power." It was the only thing that came to mind that would make sense.

And it would have worked if her son hadn't been so nosey. He reached over to the light switch and flicked it upward, illuminating the small laundry room with the light from overhead. His eyes narrowed and he crossed his arms. "Really?"

Agatha huffed, striding over to the switch to flip it off. "Yes, really. They must have gotten done with it. But there's no sense in wasting electricity, is there?" She headed back to the cupboard only to realize that it was empty except for a box of fabric softener sheets.

She could feel her son's gaze on her, drilling into her back. It wasn't hard to assume he was judging her or assuming something was up. And he would be right. Her only prayer would be for him to drop whatever it was he might think was going on with her and leave her be.

Her hand wrapped around the box and she spun to face him. "What did you need, dear?"

Thomas's eyes darted from her face to the box and back. "What do you need those for?"

Agatha lifted the box, moving it from one hand to the other. "I still have laundry to do, and Zeke doesn't have the dryer sheets I like at the cabin."

"There's a laundry room at the cabin?"

At least she didn't have to lie this time. "Of course there isn't. But there is a stacked washer and dryer in that hall closet. How do you think I've been able to keep my clothes clean? I could have sworn I showed you when I gave you the grand tour."

To his credit, Thomas looked chagrined. The cocky look he sported left his face in a flash and he broke eye contact. "I wanted to tell you that I won't be able to make dinner tonight."

"Really?" Agatha winced at the utter relief in her voice, made worse by the way Thomas shot her a surprised look.

"Yeah. I'm going to put in some extra hours. Callahan is offering overtime for anyone willing to camp out and move the cattle over to the Baker ranch temporarily. I'll only be gone one night, mostly to make sure everything is settled and there aren't any predators. You gonna be okay?"

She snorted, waving the box through the air. "I'm perfectly fine, dear. I don't need you to babysit me. This isn't the first evening we won't share a meal together, and it won't be the last. You go have fun."

"Well, I wouldn't exactly call it fun..."

"Sweetheart, it's about time that we accept you're going to be finding your own way in the world." Her stomach tightened even as the words escaped her throat. The conversation she'd had with Zeke had only made her realize just how attached Thomas was to her, and she wasn't doing him any favors by letting him continue to fret about her. She smiled, moving closer to him. "One of these days you're going to find someone to care about, and you're going to have to shift all your focus to starting your own family. It will be okay."

"You're sure you'll be okay?"

She nodded resolutely. "And when you get back, I'll have your favorite ready for dinner."

"Sloppy Joes?"

"Who do you think I am? Of course sloppy Joes." She laughed. "Now scoot. I'm sure you have a lot of work to do before you leave later." She hurried him out the door, once again relieved she didn't have to come up with a fib to keep him away.

Now all she had to worry about was what she might wear for when Zeke picked her up later.

17

Zeke

Zeke felt young again. There was something about being with Agatha that made him feel so much more alive. That wasn't to say that he'd been needing a relationship to fulfill him all these years. He knew better than to believe it was so simple.

Agatha was the reason. The way she always had a response for everything, while irritating at times, was also amusing. She had a knack for keeping him on his toes.

Zeke chuckled as he got ready for his date. This was the start of something new, something exciting, something he hadn't known he needed.

He found himself looking forward to really getting to know this woman beyond what he had discovered he liked about her already. As soon as he finished buttoning his shirt, he grabbed his hat from his bed and hurried downstairs.

The picnic basket was packed with cold-cut sandwiches, chips, and a variety of fruit. He'd put everything together while his daughters were out of the house and hid the basket near the back door.

Now all he had to do was get two horses saddled without anyone paying attention. Thankfully this was the time of day when most of his men were getting their supper. It shouldn't be too difficult to slip away unnoticed.

Turning the corner to the kitchen, Zeke froze in his place. Eloise stood by the back door hunched over the picnic basket, her brows furrowed. She glanced up, but her expression didn't change.

He couldn't move. All his plans were about to crumble to the ground. If Eloise had figured out who he was about to go see, then there was zero chance she'd keep his secret—especially from Shane.

Then that would get back to Agatha and she'd be upset with Zeke about spilling the details of their budding relationship.

It was easy to lose track of time as he stood there. Ten minutes might have passed, or it could have been only thirty seconds. All he knew was that he needed her to say something first so he could figure out what she *thought* was going on. He shifted, turning his hat over in his hands. "Well?"

"Well?" Eloise lifted a brow. "Well... are you going to tell me what you're going to be up to today? Or do I have to drag it from you?"

"I'm going on a picnic," he said simply.

"A *picnic*." She glanced down at the contents of the basket. "With wine and grapes and—"

"And sandwiches, yes. Just because a man wants to go on a picnic with wine and sandwiches doesn't mean nothin'."

She reached into the basket and pulled out two glasses, giving him a pointed look.

Zeke slapped his hat onto his head and strode forward,

taking the glasses from her and putting them back in the basket. "Doesn't mean nothin'," he muttered again.

"If you're going on a date, why didn't you tell us?"

"It's not a date."

"Dad," she drawled. "It's a *date*."

He avoided looking directly at her. "Whether it is or it isn't is none of your business. I'm going out on a picnic, and you'd be wise not to tell a soul."

She smiled as she dragged her finger and thumb in a pinched position across her lips.

"And stop looking at me like that." He flipped the basket lid shut and straightened. "Nothing is happening."

"Of course it isn't."

"And even if it was, it wouldn't be any of your business."

"Except for the fact that you made our relationships your business our entire lives." She snickered, earning herself a sharp look.

"That's different. I'm your father."

She shrugged. "It'll come out eventually. But you won't have to worry about it coming out from me. I'll keep your little secret until you're ready to share it. Just..." She tilted her head, her smile softening. "Don't go standing in your own way."

Zeke frowned. "What is that even supposed to mean?"

"I know how much you loved Mom. Don't compare anyone to her because you're never going to find someone who is anything like her. Whoever this is, if you like her, go for it." She headed out of the kitchen before he had a chance to tell her she was wrong or make up any other excuses.

He stared down at the basket for a moment, then picked it up. If this was the only drawback to tonight's date, then he'd be lucky. Thank goodness it was Eloise who caught him and not Brielle or Adeline. He had no doubt those two could do some damage with this information.

Zeke sent a quick prayer that he'd get off the property with the picnic basket and not be caught by anyone else who might take note of his behavior. He still wanted some time to himself with Agatha before they let it out in the open.

Thankfully his prayers were answered when he got into the barn and found not a single soul was hanging around. He got his horses, snuck out the back and was quickly on his way. Every step he got closer to seeing Agatha made all his insecurities fall away. There was no telling what the future would look like with her, but for the first time in a long time, he was excited to find out.

Zeke pulled his horse to a stop in front of the cabin and dismounted. The second his boots hit the ground, his heart went into overdrive. They'd spent enough time together that this official first date shouldn't be affecting him like this.

And yet it was.

He took a deep breath, blew it out through pursed lips and then gave himself a firm nod before striding forward. The cabin door opened before he got to it and Agatha materialized. Her loose-fitted white blouse was paired with a nice set of jeans that hugged her figure. But what pulled everything together and made his stomach twist like a tornado was the cowboy hat and boots she'd donned with them.

Zeke placed a hand to his heart and let out a slow whistle. "You look…"

She glanced down at her outfit, then flashed him a nervous smile. "Is it too much?"

He shook his head. "No, ma'am. You look like you were born and bred to be a cowgirl."

Her smile widened and she stepped toward him, easily placing her hands around his neck. "What can I say? I learned from the best." Her lips whispered a kiss against his. How she could manage to draw him in, lasso him to the point he didn't dare move was beyond him. This woman had already managed to capture his attention, and it would only be a matter of time before she controlled his heart.

Agatha was the first to withdraw from their kiss, leaving him aching for more. She nodded behind him to where he'd left the horses. "It's a good thing I know you, Zeke Callahan. Or I might have gone with a different option."

"Oh yeah? What option was that?"

She slipped her hand into his, and they headed for the horses. "A woman my age has two kinds of looks. She can sport a pair of jeans or get dolled up in a dress."

He stopped and faced her, anticipation already manifesting itself within. "Well, Ms. Birch, one of these days I'm going to have to see this other look you speak of."

Her coy smile only served to add to the way he was feeling.

They stopped at the horses, and her eyes flitted to meet his. "A picnic?"

"I thought you said you knew me," he teased.

"I only meant that you wouldn't be caught dead in a fancy restaurant—especially at one of those in town."

Zeke's eyes narrowed. "You didn't eat supper already, did you?"

"Of course not."

"Then what did you suppose we were going to be doing? I told you I'd take you to dinner."

She flushed that pretty rose color he found so irresistible. "I suppose I didn't know what I was expecting. Perhaps you'd take us to your place."

He threw his head back and laughed. "I'm not in the business of telling anyone about my personal life. And if my daughters knew I was dating, I wouldn't hear the end of it." His expression grew serious, and he pulled her closer as his voice lowered. "No, I want to spend this evening with you and only you. I don't need to share you with anyone, and that's how I like it."

Agatha placed her hand against his cheek. "Who knew you could be such a charmer?"

"I only share this side of me with the women I care about, so count yourself lucky."

"Oh, I do," she insisted, then she kissed him again.

The sparks of electricity that came with each peck hadn't faded, no matter how many times she touched him. This was a strange new experience he wasn't prepared for, and yet he was ready to dive right in.

Zeke held up her hand as she placed her toe into the stirrup. "I have the perfect spot for our picnic. You're going to love it."

"I don't doubt it." The way she gazed down at him like he was the only man in the world set off a wave of fireworks. He could stand there all day looking up at her and be content.

She let out a little laugh and touched her hair. "What?"

He shook his head. "Nothing."

The ride wasn't long. In fact, the clearing was just on the other side of where he'd pitched his tent, but when they took the scenic route, he could continue to sneak glances at her.

Once the picnic was all set up and they were seated on the blanket, it was almost too easy to fall into conversation.

Agatha took a bite of her sandwich and closed her eyes with pleasure. "Do you know how long it's been since I've had a good turkey sandwich?"

He chuckled. "Flattery will get you everywhere."

"Oh, I know." She grinned at him as she plucked a piece of lettuce that dangled from her sandwich. "I'm well aware of your ego."

He scoffed. "My ego?"

"Sure. You run the largest ranch in the area."

"More like in the state."

She gave him that look—the one that said this was what she meant—and he chuckled again.

"Okay, you got me. Continue."

This time Agatha laughed. "And as such, you have the largest staff on hand to take care of it. You are in charge of so many lives and their family's well-being."

"Go on."

She gave him a playful shove. "And yet you're spending every day at my home rebuilding the life I lost." Her voice got quieter, more serious. "Why is that?"

He hadn't expected to feel so on the spot with this one.

"I've been over it in my head again and again," she added.

Zeke cleared his throat, drawing her focus. "I would think it's obvious. I like you."

She wrinkled her nose. "Boy, that wasn't the reason when you started."

She was right. Agatha was the kind of person who came at him like a boomerang. But there was something he hadn't expected even in the beginning.

"You didn't strike me as the kind of woman who would have just given up."

"Okay..." she drawled. "But that doesn't explain why you would go out of your way to help me."

Was she expecting him to say something that would put him in a bad light? It was the only thing that made sense to his muddled brain. He didn't know what she was trying to get from him.

He shifted uncomfortably for a moment, then understanding flooded his mind. "Do you remember when we went back to the site to find your pictures?"

"Yes."

"There was something about that day... I just knew I needed to be the one to help you over that hurdle. You would have figured it out, I'm sure of it. But... I just knew..." His voice trailed off. How could he tell her that he'd practically been pushed into helping, and he couldn't quite remember what it was that had been the catalyst? He'd sound crazy.

Perhaps he already did.

"Maybe I knew that you were just stubborn enough that you'd get yourself into trouble if I wasn't there to rope you in."

Amusement flickered over her face. and the relief that consumed him over getting through this part of the conversation eased the ache in his chest. She shook her head. "I'm not the one who would get herself into trouble. I can handle myself."

"You say that a lot," he said.

"You don't believe me?"

He snorted. "Besides some of my daughters, there aren't many single women I've met who can truly take care of themselves—"

"Hey!" Agatha threw a grape at him.

"You didn't let me finish!" He laughed as he retrieved the missile and popped it into his mouth. "But if anyone has come close, it's you."

She tilted her head—that look once again on her face that made him feel like he could do anything. "Thank you... I think."

"No thanks needed. It's the truth."

"It must have really been hard raising so many headstrong women."

"You have *no* idea. If they even knew what I was up to tonight... there would be no end to the prodding and questions. Count yourself lucky you only have the one."

"Thomas is wonderful. I was truly blessed with him." Her eyes got a far-off look and she picked less at the food she held in her hand.

"And his father?"

Her eyes bounced to meet his, then dropped. She didn't

even attempt to meet his gaze as she picked at the crumbs on the blanket. "What about him?"

Zeke hesitated. This kind of conversation wasn't the best to have on a first date. They probably should be keeping things light.

When she lifted her eyes once more, he knew he needed to just push through.

"Was he present?"

"Not in the slightest."

Zeke didn't know what he'd expected Agatha to say. He'd figured the man would have been involved at least a little through Thomas's childhood. But nothing? The thought sent an insidious tremor through his body. A man needed to be there for his family. It didn't matter that they'd separated; it was his duty to raise his boy right. "What do you mean?"

"Exactly how it sounds. Thomas's father didn't raise him. Honestly, it was a good thing he wasn't around. I get the sense he would have been more trouble than he was worth. He had a drinking problem and a drug problem. And a... yelling problem."

That tremor from before only grew stronger. She wasn't inferring that her ex was abusive, was she? His free hand balled into a fist, but then Agatha placed hers over it.

"It's fine. He passed away a few years ago. I don't much care for dredging up those memories. I'm just glad I was able to leave with my self-worth intact."

18

Agatha

"You shouldn't have had to go through any of that," Zeke said.

Agatha focused on her hand that still covered Zeke's rather than meeting his gaze. Even after all these years, she'd never told anyone exactly how hard it had been being married to Thomas's father.

As much as she would have liked to forget everything she went through, she knew she never would. The scars left behind by the way he treated her emotionally were many. But at least those experiences were enough to pull her out of the darkness and help her fight for the future. "I will never regret or resent that I had to go through any of it." This time she did meet his gaze. "Those experiences were what helped me realize I could only count on myself. And perhaps they're the reason why Thomas and I are so close."

Zeke stiffened. "You had to lie to him about what you were doing tonight."

Her lips curled into a half-smile. "Actually, I didn't. Everything worked out for the best. Turns out you played a big part in it, too."

His brows furrowed and he inched closer. "I'm sorry, I don't know what you mean."

Agatha laced her fingers through his, tracing her thumb on the back of his hand. "Well, you have that overnight cattle run or something. He volunteered to help. So he said he couldn't make it. I guess things seem to work out for us in ways we don't expect more often than we realize."

"What overnight cattle thing?"

She glanced at him before she tugged her hand free to reach for her wine glass. "I don't know. It's your ranch. He said you were looking for more men to keep an eye on the cattle at a new pasture or something. I don't know all of it. But it sounded pretty perfect to me. Did you plan that part too?" Her smile stretched wider at the thought of Zeke creating a job just so she wouldn't have to lie to her son.

While misguided, it was still romantic.

"There's no overnight cattle drive, Agatha."

"What are you talking about? He stopped by and told me himself."

"I don't know what to tell you. My cattle are right where they should be and won't be moved for another couple of days."

She stared at him, unseeing. His words didn't make sense. It was like he was speaking another language altogether. "What do you mean they won't be moved? Thomas said—"

"Thomas lied, Agatha," he whispered.

It felt like she'd been punched in the gut. What reason would Thomas have for telling her a lie like that? He could have just as easily told her he didn't want to come to dinner. Her thoughts swirled with the unknown. He was somewhere out in the world, and she didn't know where he was.

"Hey, you okay?"

Agatha shook her head. "No. I'm not. Do you think I should call him?"

He didn't answer right away, causing her to finally look at him.

"I'm sorry. Of course not. He's an adult. He certainly doesn't need to tell me where he's going to be twenty-four-seven." But Thomas had never lied to her before.

Or had he?

Already she could feel herself going through a tailspin. The logical part of her knew that one day Thomas would move forward with his life. She'd been prepared for that. At least she thought she was.

"Agatha," Zeke said quietly, dragging her to the present. "You don't look okay."

She forced a laugh. "I'm fine. It's nothing. Thomas just told me he couldn't make it to dinner because he was working for you. But clearly that isn't happening because you have no reason to lie to me about where your men are doing their jobs."

Zeke studied her. It was as if his scrutiny was able to tear away all the layers she had put in place, and now she was as vulnerable as a rosebud in a winter storm. She shivered with the thought and pushed through the confusion and mild feeling of betrayal.

This was a date—a very sweet date with a man she had been looking forward to seeing all day. She wasn't going to put aside that excitement because her son had chosen to lie to her about what he was up to.

Agatha placed her hand over Zeke's again and lifted her eyes to meet his. "I'm fine. Just a little thrown off."

He didn't look convinced, but what else could she say?

"My daughters hid stuff from me too."

She waved her hand dismissively. "It's *fine.*"

"No, it's not. You're worried about him. I can tell."

Agatha sighed. "Yes, I'm worried about him. I don't know

where he is. But he's twenty. He can do what he wants to do on his time, and he'll just tell me about it later."

"Adeline, my oldest, lied about being pregnant by a man I didn't even think she liked."

She stared at Zeke, her eyes wide. Then she let out a laugh. She clapped a hand over her mouth, but it was too late. The damage had been done, and all she could do was pray that Zeke wouldn't think that she was making fun of him. "I'm sorry, I didn't mean—"

He held up a hand. "Don't worry about it. She was set on marrying a man that I didn't approve of—but not because there was anything wrong with him. He was just one of the young men in town I didn't think was good enough for my little girl."

His words tugged at her heartstrings. She'd rarely seen this gentler side of Zeke, and right here, she was melting over a story he probably didn't look back on fondly.

"Turns out she was just trying to get married quickly because she wanted to give her sisters the chance to be up next." Zeke looked away, rubbing the back of his neck. The chagrined expression he wore said it all. He wasn't ready to share his flaws with her. And she had a feeling he was going to come forward with the details she'd already heard from the people in town.

"Before you moved here, I was a little... strict."

She bit back a smile.

"I told the girls that the younger ones couldn't be married without the older ones doing it first. I figured it would make it easier on me to have to only vet one at a time." He blew out a long breath and then a forced chuckle. "Boy, was I wrong—on *so* many levels. Those girls have managed to turn me upside down and inside out without even trying."

"I'm sure they still loved you all the same," she said.

He met her gaze and shook his head. "Yeah, I know they love me. But I didn't treat them in such a way that showed I loved them. I wanted to protect them from the young men out there that only wanted one thing." Zeke looked away again, and she wanted to assure him that she thought he'd done just fine raising all of his girls. But anything she might have said would have sounded trite. Finally, he met her gaze. "I guess what I'm trying to say is that I came to realize just how important it is to let them make their own mistakes. I did the best I could, raising them. Now it's their turn to get out in the world and be on their own." He chuckled again, but this time it was less strained. "Only I'm still stuck with half of them. But that's what you get when you have a family ranch and most of them still help out."

She squeezed his hand. "I don't know how you managed to do it and keep your wits about you. Honestly, I feel like girls are so much harder than boys. Thomas has always been this golden child. In school he always got good grades. He never snuck out to be with his friends... he's always told me every-thing." Until now.

"I'm sure he's just working through something, and he doesn't want to worry you."

She groaned. "But that's when parents worry the most."

They met one another's eyes and both smiled. If they had anything in common, it was this. They had both raised their children on their own for the most part. And they still worried about them. Her thoughts shifted back to when Zeke had told her why he was out in the woods camping rather than being at home. How it had felt different and crowded but also empty at the same time.

Now she understood. Their lives were changing in ways neither one of them was prepared for. But maybe it wasn't so bad. They were moving on to better things.

Perhaps that included each other.

She wrapped her fingers around his, loving the worn callouses that showed just how hard he'd worked over the years. Every scar, every mark that told his story only added to how she viewed him. Her thumb traced over one such mark on his hand, and she glanced at Zeke. "Tell me about this one."

He glanced down to where she rubbed at a spot near his wrist. "Oh, that's an old one."

It had turned white, no longer the angry red coloring that most scars presented with. She trailed her fingertip along the two-inch-long mark. "Do you remember?"

Zeke captured her hand in his. He laced her fingers between his own and nodded. "I was about eleven."

She lifted her brows.

"We had this mean old mare that hated getting her girth tightened. But she was an excellent horse to ride once she was all saddled and ready to go."

"Don't tell me..."

Zeke brought her hand to his lips and brushed a kiss along her knuckles. "Yep. That mean old mare took a bite out of me."

She gasped. "What happened?"

He gave her a funny look. "What do you think? I got it bandaged up and went for my ride."

Laughter spilled from her lips. "No, what happened to that mare? You didn't put her down, did you?"

This time he stared at her like she'd grown antlers and started doing a jig. "Why would I do a dumb thing like that?"

She flushed. "Because she bit an eleven-year-old boy."

"That horse was the best horse by a long shot when it came to working my dad's ranch. It would have been a poor business decision to get rid of her for her attitude. With that logic, we should send you out to pasture."

Agatha gasped. "Excuse me?"

He chuckled. "You're just about as stubborn and mean as that mare was."

"I've never bitten you!" she exclaimed.

"Yet."

She gaped at him. Then she couldn't control herself. Her

laughter echoed through the trees, sending birds and other critters fleeing from their quiet sanctuary.

"I guess you better be careful then. You never know when a gal like me could turn on you." Her tone was lighthearted, but when she met his gaze, she sobered.

The way he stared at her once again threw her off. His steady gaze drilled into her as if he could see all of her secrets, all of her flaws—everything that made her human. She blinked but couldn't tear her focus from him even if she tried.

Zeke cocked his head slightly, his attention never wavering. "You are something else, Agatha Birch."

Her mouth went dry, and it didn't matter how many times she tried to swallow; it felt like it was full of sand.

"You just keep surprising me," he said.

"How so," she rasped, not certain she wanted to hear what he had to say but at the same time craving to know exactly what he thought of her.

"You raised a boy all on your own. You have a career, and you don't take flak from anyone. I've never seen someone so strong-willed before."

"I thought you hated that about me?"

His soft voice broke as he let out a chuckle. "Yeah, well, perhaps it's growing on me."

She smiled. "Perhaps you're growing on me, too."

"I'd like to keep seeing you."

"I wouldn't have it any other way." Warmth spread like wildfire within her. This was the start of something amazing. She could feel it. They might have gotten off to a rocky start, but she could see a future with this man—and it didn't terrify her nearly as much as she thought it would.

Her ex might have been controlling and borderline abusive. But not every man was like him. Zeke was different. He was thoughtful and generous. There was a quiet kind of peacefulness about him that drew her to him in an unexpected way.

For the first time in a long while, she was excited and looking forward to her future.

When their picnic was all cleaned up, Zeke took her by the hand and they wandered along the edges of the clearing. Neither one of them spoke as darkness fell. The sunset wasn't even the best part because as soon as the stars came out, they were surrounded by a sky full of glitter.

Agatha leaned into Zeke, glancing up at him every so often and finding him admiring the sky. He had a gentle soul. She could sense it. Once upon a time she had thought she'd spend the rest of her life alone—with only Thomas to care for.

That had suddenly changed.

Maybe second chances at love were possible. People just had to find the one that could make them whole again.

They rode the horses back to the cabin, and Zeke kissed her goodnight. She watched him ride off with both horses until the darkness swallowed him, then she closed the door and rested against it.

A sigh of pleasure burst from her lips, and she let out a little laugh. Her fingertips touched the still tender skin where he'd kissed her, and she marveled at how easy it was to find herself falling in love with a man she'd thought too brash and controlling. There was so much more to him than she had realized, and all of her misgivings were now falling away.

Rather than be concerned about her growing feelings for Zeke, she had other things to worry about.

Namely, Thomas and what he was up to.

19

Zeke

Zeke's date couldn't have gone any better if he had weeks to plan it. Were there hiccups? Sure. Eloise knew there was something up and she could spill every bit of it. There was no telling what his other daughters would say or do if they found out, and he had to hope that they'd just mind their own business. He got home late enough to put the horses back in their stalls without being noticed.

And now all he had to do was look forward to the next date.

He didn't bother returning to his campsite after bringing the horses back and opted to stay in his own room. It was strange waking up in his own bed after spending so many nights in the woods, but that wasn't the worst of it.

The second he got to the kitchen for breakfast, several pairs of surprised eyes pinned him to his place. Eloise, Brielle, Grace, and Adeline were seated at the kitchen table eating breakfast. Adeline was the only one who still lived here with her husband since they ran most of the daily events. Brielle still handled a good deal of work at the ranch, too. But Grace and Eloise had their own jobs.

Immediately, his gaze landed on Eloise. He frowned at her even in his attempt to keep his features schooled. "I thought after you were all married off, you'd be living your own lives. What are you doing eating breakfast at home?"

Eloise glanced toward Brielle, who grinned from ear to ear.

Zeke groaned. "I thought you weren't going to tell anyone."

"What?" Eloise laughed. "Brielle dragged it from me. It's not my fault."

He shoved his hands into his pockets and trudged toward the coffee maker. "You didn't have to say a thing."

"Who is she, Dad?" Brielle called from her seat at the table. "She must be pretty special for you to put together a picnic for her."

"And take two horses out for an evening ride," Adeline joined in.

He shot a sharp look at her. "How did you know?"

His eldest daughter rolled her eyes. "Come on, Dad. The horses were clearly taken out. If I didn't notice details like that, you wouldn't want me running the ranch."

Grace was the only one who hadn't commented yet. She seemed to just be present for the gossip. Of course. That was what this was about.

Zeke sighed and dragged a hand down his face. "You might as well all give it a rest. I'm not going to spill a single drop of that honey you're after. So go on your way. I'm sure you all have better things to do than to sit around here and try to figure out who I fancy."

"Oooh. You hear that? He fancies someone," Brielle crooned. "Seems to me that the world has come full circle. Dad's found himself a girl, and now he wants to be left alone. I don't think he deserves his privacy on this one. What do you think?"

Adeline and Eloise seemed to give each other a knowing smile, but Grace was still watching him quietly.

He leaned against the counter, his coffee cup in hand. "You're not getting anything from me. You have your own lives to worry about."

"Not even a hint? Is it someone we know? Or how about you tell us how far it's gotten. Are we going to have a new mother?" Brielle's teasing was getting out of hand.

"We know it's serious because he took the good wine with him," Eloise pointed out.

"I don't care who it is, as long as he's happy." Adeline got to her feet, her smile still plastered to her face. She headed across the room and stood on her toes to kiss his cheek. "I hope she's everything you deserve," she said. "I'm going to get to work, and the rest of you should too."

"You're no fun!" Brielle tossed at her as Adeline left the room.

"She's right, guys. Let Dad have his moment. When he's ready, he'll tell us." Grace's soft words finally filled the quiet room. Her small smile said more than even those words could express. She nodded toward him, then gathered her dishes and took them to the sink. "Everyone deserves to find love. And some of us are lucky enough to find it more than once, right, Dad?"

He wouldn't go so far as to say he was in *love*. At least he wouldn't have said as much before last night, but he'd connected with Agatha more than he'd expected.

"Dad?" Grace murmured.

He jumped, then grunted. "Right." Putting his mug aside, he nodded toward his remaining daughters and headed toward the door.

It wasn't until he heard the hurried footsteps that he noted Grace had followed him. Her steps were quick and quiet, but she didn't say anything even when she fell into step beside him.

They made it all the way to the entrance of the barn before he faced her.

"Is there something you wanted, Grace?"

She glanced back at the house and then up at him. "Don't worry about Brielle and Eloise. They're just happy for you, that's all."

He bit back a smile. "You've always been the peacekeeper of the family, but you don't have to worry about me. I'm not upset."

Her eyes narrowed, but the motion was almost too small to notice. "But you're not wanting to share any information with us."

Zeke placed a hand on her shoulder and squeezed it gently. "I don't need to tell you everything. You are all adults, and you all have your own lives now."

"But that doesn't change the fact that you're still our dad. We worry about you just as much as you worry about us. We always will."

Her words weighed down on him, bringing him back to reality. Since he'd told all the girls they had the freedom to choose who they dated and when they wanted to get married, Zeke had distanced himself from them—more than he should have. He'd let them take the reins and run with them.

In that time, he'd lost track of the relationships he had with them. They were practically strangers to him now. He nodded, peering out at the expanse of his property to keep himself from getting emotional. "Well, then you'd be thrilled to know that I'm doing great—better than great. The woman I'm seeing is amazing. You'd really like her."

"I'm sure I will." Grace moved forward and gave him a tight hug around his middle. "When you're ready to introduce her to us, I'll be the first to say so."

He hugged her back, his thoughts shifting to Agatha and what it might look like to not only share her with his daughters but the other way around. A smile touched his lips as he rested his chin on her head. He really needed to do better at touching base with his daughters. They might be adults now, but they'd always need him. "Thanks," he whispered. "When we get to that point, I'll be sure to let you know first that it's happening."

Grace pulled away. "Good. I have to get back to the club so I can get ready for some sessions. I'll see you at dinner? I think Eloise planned on making something."

"You girls need to worry about your own husbands and not your old man."

"Dad," she murmured with exasperation.

Zeke nodded. "Fine, I'll be home for dinner."

She smiled, then headed toward the cars parked at the house. His daughters had all grown up so much over the past few years, and he'd missed some of it because of his own insecurities. It was time to get back to who he was before—a man who knew when to bring up something that needed to be dealt with.

Like Thomas Birch.

He turned toward the barn. Thomas was usually already up and getting stuff done. He was a hard worker and someone Zeke found far more dependable than he would have originally expected.

Thomas had impressed him enough to earn a more coveted position at the ranch, but based on what Agatha had mentioned last night, the young man needed a talking to.

There was just one problem.

Zeke's steps faltered.

If he brought up the conversation with Agatha, then Thomas would know about their relationship. Agatha didn't want that.

Zeke stopped, stared at the barn, then in the direction of his hunting cabin. He was torn. Agatha needed him, and yet his hands were tied.

Just as he had decided he'd drop the issue, Thomas materialized from the barn. He stopped suddenly, then glanced behind him as if he expected Zeke to be looking for someone else entirely. His head swiveled back around and he took a small step forward. "Were you looking for someone, Mr. Callahan?"

Zeke didn't know what came over him. It might have very well been his protective nature finally being unearthed from the hole he'd tried to bury it in. He strode forward so quickly that Thomas took a short step backward.

"A word, Mr. Birch."

The young man blinked several times, then nodded as he followed Zeke around the side of the barn. This early in the morning, Zeke didn't think he'd be overheard, but he thought it better to be safe than sorry. The last thing he needed was Eloise or Brielle walking in on him having a discussion about Thomas's whereabouts.

Zeke spun around and faced Thomas once they were far enough away from anyone who might cross paths with them. "I need you to clarify something for me, son."

Thomas blinked a few more times, straightened his shoulders then nodded firmly. "Yes, sir. What do you need?"

"Where were you last night?"

The confidence drained from the young man's face. He blinked a few more times, then looked away. "Sir?"

"Last night. In the evening after your shift, where were you?"

"I don't... I'm not sure how that is any of your business." His eyes flitted up to meet Zeke's, then flew away just as fast as the timid bird he seemed to have become. "Sir," he amended.

"I think it is very much my business seeing as you are using my name to spread lies."

All at once, the young man's gaze cut to Zeke's. The confusion, guilt, and even some accusation flooded his countenance, but he didn't argue.

"I'm guessing you're wondering how I would know that you lied to your mother about where you were going to be."

"You'd be correct in that." Thomas's voice had turned guarded. He wasn't about to give anything away that he didn't have to, and his suspicions were going up by the second.

"As you're probably aware, your mother has been working a great deal on your home—much to my displeasure." Adding that last bit might help him brush off any accusations Thomas would throw at him. "She's also a talker who shares far more than she ought to. After you couldn't make dinner, she told me about it. Imagine my surprise when she told me that I assigned you to do some overtime on a job that didn't need doing."

Thomas blanched. "Sir, I—"

"I'm sorry, son. But I don't lie, and when your mother mentioned it, I *did* confirm that I don't have any wranglers watching the cattle. She's aware that you lied to her." Zeke didn't think that Thomas could pale any more than he already had. He looked positively ghost-like.

"I didn't lie because I was up to no good. I want you to know that."

"I don't care what the lie was about. I care that it happened in the first place. I don't hire dishonest folk around here." Zeke swallowed down the bile that seemed to rise with his own uttered lie.

His brows shot up and he squirmed. "Are you going to fire me? I swear I wasn't trying to do anything wrong. I needed to go to the city, and I wasn't going to get there in time if I had to make it to supper with my mother."

What on earth did the kid need to go to the city for that he wanted to hide from his mother? Before he could voice that question, Thomas continued.

"I met a girl."

And then everything shifted back into place. The kid had a girlfriend—in the city, no less. Zeke could only imagine what kind of conversation that would entail with Agatha. She'd moved out here to be with her son. And now he was interested in someone who could take him away from all of this—that, or it would force Agatha to distance herself from her only family.

Zeke's heart bottomed out.

That wasn't a possibility, was it? She'd come all the way out to Copper Creek just so she could stay close to her son. If he were to find love in the city and move back, then what did that mean for Agatha?

"Please don't fire me. I'll tell my mother—"

Zeke held up a hand, cutting the kid off. If he could just have a little more time with Agatha before Thomas confessed everything, maybe Agatha would consider staying in Copper Creek for good. She could find additional family here—with him. "Don't go spilling the beans on my account. I'm sure there's a reason you kept this information from your mother."

Thomas nodded but didn't divulge the information.

"Whatever that reason is, it isn't any of my business. Whatever relationship you have with your mother is between the two of you. I would suggest, however, that you ease her concerns by telling her something with at least a degree of truth. Otherwise, I'm never going to hear the end of it for the next week."

Zeke rubbed his hand along the stubble on his face and shot one more look toward Thomas before he brushed past him. He prayed this wasn't going to bite him when it inevitably came full circle. Truly, this little secret wasn't his business. Agatha probably wouldn't have even wanted him to have this conversation with her son in the first place.

That truth alone was enough to help him push the concern to the side. He still had time with her before everything would come out. And if he worked fast, then she wouldn't have to worry about her son moving back to the city.

He glanced at his watch, noting he'd be late for breakfast if he didn't head out to the cabin in the next five minutes. And that wasn't something he was willing to risk. With a whistle on his lips, Zeke headed over to his ATV and started the engine. He couldn't wait to pull that woman into his arms and kiss her like he'd never see her again. That was the kind of thing a man did when he was in love.

There. He'd admitted it.

Zeke Callahan had fallen in love again.

And her name was Agatha Birch.

20

───────

Agatha

gatha felt itchy all over. It wasn't the regular kind of itch, like from a bug bite or an allergy. Something had shifted in her life, and not in a good way.

Well, there were good things shifting as well. Zeke's kind eyes had fed her dreams all night long, and if it weren't for the concerns she had over Thomas's lies, she might have been humming a little tune as she got breakfast ready for the two of them.

Thomas hadn't called or checked in—though she realized he wouldn't have done so if he was working anyway. That was why she couldn't call him this morning to check in herself. He'd know she was on to him, and if he knew that, there was no telling where that conversation would go.

It could be an argument, or it might turn into something even worse. What if he piled onto the lies even more?

Smoke filled the room and she gasped as she stared down at the pan she'd been frying eggs in. She grabbed the handle and removed the pan from the small stove, but the smoke still filled the room.

Half expecting the smoke detectors to go off, she glanced around only to discover there were none. Well, that was concerning. What about forest fires?

She shook her head. There were more important things to worry about at this moment. The food was burning, the cabin was filling with the stench of smoke, Zeke would be arriving any moment for breakfast, and she still didn't know what could prompt her son to lie to her after twenty years.

A knock on the door yanked her from her spiraling thoughts, which had tugged her down further and further.

Another knock.

Agatha lurched into action. "One second!" She grabbed a hand towel, then rushed for the window and flung it open before she whacked the rag through the air to force the smoke to leave the cabin.

Zeke's muttered curse was easily heard through the open window, and the knob rattled. He knocked again, calling, "Agatha, open this door. Is everything okay?"

Heat seared her face. Shoot! His frantic calls might have been endearing if this wasn't his own cabin and she hadn't just burned his breakfast.

"I'm fine!" she called back. "Just got distracted."

Keys jingled, and she shouldn't have been surprised when he flung open the door and strode inside. He almost looked more like a hulking grizzly rather than the sweet cowboy from the night before. His eyes swept through the room, landing on the still-smoking pan of food. Without warning, he strode forward, grabbed the pan, and dumped its contents in the sink. With a flip of his hand, he started the water running. "What in heaven's name happened here?"

Her blush only grew hotter. "I'm so sorry. I was cooking and I got distracted and—"

"You could have been hurt."

She snapped her mouth shut.

"What if that fire had caught on something else?"

"It wasn't a fire," she insisted.

"There was smoke."

"Yes, but it wasn't on fire. It was just... smokey. I was perfectly safe, I assure you."

He stared at her with hard eyes. She remembered those eyes. They were the same accusatory eyes from when he'd found her at her house when it was still smoking. Agatha brushed off that thought. When she'd met him, he'd been unwilling to listen to reason. He'd grown so much since then. He wasn't going to revert to the person he once was.

"The eggs got burnt. That's all. I'm fine, but the eggs are ruined—clearly—so I'm fixing us up some new ones." She took the pan from him, her fingers grazing his. The spark from his touch was still very much alive, and her eyes jumped to meet his in that moment.

His blues smoldered like there was a fire that licked at him just beneath the surface. All at once she was able to forget the worries from the night before. Just being with Zeke like this— like they were something more, felt so right. She exhaled, and that was it.

Zeke placed his hands on her waist. She gasped, the pan clattering to the sink so she could get a good grip around his neck. "Why is it that I can't stop thinking about you?" he said. "I can't stop remembering the way you feel in my arms or worrying about you out here all alone."

"I'm not alone," she whispered. "You're not far at all."

His lips quirked upward. "You make a good point. One of these days, you're going to get tired of that fact."

"I don't think that's possible."

Zeke looked at her upturned face. "You better be right." He dipped his face toward hers, capturing her lips in a firm, unyielding kiss. This one was different than all the others somehow. She couldn't put her finger on it, but something had changed. He was more brash, more demanding. It was like he'd finally realized that she was all in and he wanted to show her just how much she meant to him.

Her heart reacted to that thought as if it had caught fire, too. The room spun, hotter and hotter as she let herself give in to this man. Their kiss deepened, and the world itself disappeared. They might have completely lost themselves if it weren't for an incessant buzzing.

At first, she tried to ignore it, and she might have been successful if Zeke hadn't pulled away and looked for the source.

Agatha stumbled a step, and Zeke had to hold onto her upper arm to help steady her. When she got control of her bearings, she looked around the room and located her phone next to the stove. She gave him a playful smile and held up a finger. "Hold that thought."

With quick and yet unsteady steps, she hurried toward her phone and picked it up. Thomas's image populated the screen and reality crashed over her like a bucket of ice water, extinguishing all the fire that had just erupted around her.

She placed the phone to her ear. "Thomas? Is everything all right?" So many scenarios played in her head. He was hurt. He was stranded. Something terrible had happened and now he was locked up in county.

"I'm fine, Mom. But I need to talk to you about something."

At some point, Zeke had found his way back to her and had wrapped his arms around her waist, pulling her back against his chest. She sucked in sharply, stifling her urge to gasp or giggle. "What are you doing calling me so early? You never do that."

"I know. I'm sorry."

"Sorry about what? Calling me so early? Are you *sure* you're okay?"

Zeke held her in his arms, and she squeezed her eyes shut as if that would be enough for her to focus on what her son was saying. She leaned in against Zeke but then thought better of it and pulled away, holding up that finger again and mouthing the word, "Thomas."

He stopped, his expression sobering.

Guilt immediately accosted her. She was torn between her son and the man whose kisses she would willingly drown from. Agatha turned away from Zeke and bit down on her cheek hard enough to draw blood. Brief clarity filled her mind as she waited for an answer.

"I'm fine..." he repeated. "Are you sure *you're* okay? You sound out of breath."

She grimaced and then forced a laugh. "I'm just caught a little off guard. You said you wanted to tell me something?"

There was a small pause. It was long enough that she might have thought he hung up on her, except she could hear male voices in the background coming and going. Finally, he put her out of her misery and spoke up. "I wasn't entirely honest with you last night. I wasn't going on a work trip."

Agatha was speechless for one of the first times in her life. This was unexpected. Thomas had lied to her face and come to confess all in under twenty-four hours. She didn't dare ask him the truth; something told her that it would scare him off and start a fight. On top of that, she wasn't sure they *wouldn't* argue. She still felt betrayed by him.

"I know it wasn't right. I shouldn't have told you I was working."

Was that it? Was he seriously going to tell her he'd lied and not tell her what he was actually doing? She burned with the need to know what was going on. What was so important to him that he felt he had to lie to her?

"I know you will probably want to know where I really was or why I wasn't at home."

Yep. Agatha wanted to know *everything*. She burned to know every last scintillating detail. It had to be good. His first lie just had to be.

"The thing is…" His voice trailed off. "I don't know if I'm ready to talk about it."

"What?" she finally blurted. Her voice was sharp and a few octaves above what she normally used. "You can't just come confess to me about lying and expect me to be okay with not knowing the truth. You lost that privilege the second you chose to be dishonest."

"I knew you wouldn't be okay with it. I don't even know why I called. It was a bad idea."

Before she could say anything to his statement, he hung up the phone. She gaped at her own device in her hand, willing it to light up with another call and another apology.

What had gotten into her son?

Zeke gently pried the phone out of her hand, and in the process, she nearly shoved him aside to retrieve it. "I have to call him back."

"Why?" He put it on the counter behind him and blocked her ability to retrieve it.

Agatha lunged for it anyway. "That was Thomas. He was calling to tell me he lied about last night."

Zeke didn't react in the way she expected. She'd hoped he would be just as flustered or upset about this situation as she was. Instead, his flat expression showed nothing. Not one emotion she could read.

She tried again to get her phone. "You're not going to believe this, but not only did he tell me he didn't tell the truth, he said he wasn't ready to tell me where he really was. I don't get it. What was the point in confessing then? So he could torture me?"

"Obviously not."

Agatha shot him a death glare. "Oh yeah? When did you become an expert on young men?"

He lifted a brow and crossed his arms. "I don't think you really want me to answer that question."

Her eyes swept over his form, and the reality of this conversation sunk in. He had been a young man once upon a time. Fighting back the embarrassment, she crossed her arms and glared at him. "Okay, if you're so smart, then why did he lie? Hmm? Can you tell me why he would lie, then confess to lying but not tell me the truth?"

It was small—like the flickering of a star burning out in the distant night. But she saw it. There was some hesitancy or guilt or something he hid behind that mask he wore. Granted, she was full of hot, wired emotion and she might just be seeing things, but if she was right, Zeke knew something and he wasn't willing to clue her in.

Was this some kind of boys' club? They all wanted to keep their secrets from her now?

Agatha tapped her foot. "Well? Tell me, what good reason did he have to do any of that?"

"I can't say."

Her brows shot up and she let out a sharp bark of laughter. "He *told* you?"

Zeke stiffened. "What? Of course not. I only meant that men lie for different reasons. They do it to keep people safe. They do it out of love. They do it because... well, frankly, Agatha, we're a pretty stupid lot."

Her hands dropped to her sides.

"I really don't believe he lied with any malicious intent. It's more likely that he wanted to keep something from you to either protect you or himself from something you wouldn't approve of."

"Well, that's exactly what I'm worried about," she said.

"I know this isn't going to help... but don't be."

She snorted. "Don't be worried? Have you *met* me?"

He chuckled and moved closer to her. "Thomas is an adult. He's gotta make his own decisions and do them for reasons he believes in. He's going to come to crossroads in his life where he's going to have to decide which path he needs to take in order to make certain people happy."

Agatha peeked up at Zeke. As much as she wanted to argue with him and tell him he was wrong, she knew better. Thomas was a grown man and would need to follow his own path. Moving to Copper Creek to be close to him wasn't supposed to be her maintaining control over her son.

She just wanted to make sure they didn't grow apart.

And that was exactly what this felt like. There was a thread that had tied her son to her when he was born. At some point it had been severed, and now she was stuck wondering if and how he would find his way back to her.

Zeke's arms wrapped around her, pulling her close to him and sharing his warmth. She shivered even though she wasn't chilled at all. The irony that she now had a different man to lean on in her worries wasn't lost on her.

Eventually her son would come back to her. Their relationship would grow stronger in spite of this little bump in the road. But until then, she could focus a little more on the relationship directly in front of her.

She twisted her head around and gazed up at the man who had settled her heart. "Zeke?"

"Hmm?"

"I want to say something, but I'm not sure how you're going to react." His arms seemed to tighten around her even as he leaned back enough to get a good look at her face.

"You can tell me anything," he assured her.

"I think I'm falling for you."

He didn't move or speak right away. Her heart tripped over

itself like a clumsy newborn animal. She shouldn't have said it. Too soon. This was all too soon.

Her body revolted along with her thoughts and she attempted to pull away from him, but his hold on her remained. "I'm sorry. I shouldn't have—"

"Agatha," he said, stopping her struggle.

She still couldn't bring herself to gaze into his eyes.

"I love you, too."

Her head snapped up and she gaped at him. "Really?"

"I wouldn't lie about something like this," he whispered.

She rested her cheek against his chest. "Good. Me neither."

21

———

Zeke

Bittersweet.

That was the only way Zeke could describe how he felt about his growing feelings for Agatha. There was so much about her that he wouldn't have thought he could ever learn to tolerate, like her incessant need to do things herself when any normal woman would have accepted help.

They still butted heads over different issues when it came to the rebuild of her home. It wouldn't have mattered if four weeks or four months had passed. They still wouldn't be able to agree on things such as ordering the projects to make a job easier or safer.

Arguments over certain tools and how to use them also occurred, and he was constantly reminded how capable she was. On top of those stressors, he had a secret he was keeping from her, and every day that secret weighed on him more and more. Thomas still hadn't mentioned why he had lied to his mother, and for the time being it appeared they'd decided to forget the incident had happened.

It might have been difficult for anyone who didn't know Agatha well to see how much it still bothered her to not know what was going on. But Zeke could. He could almost feel how heavy her heart was, how distrustful she was whenever her son spoke to her. If Zeke wasn't so worried about Agatha choosing her family over him, he might have just spilled the beans to get it over with. Except this wasn't even his secret to tell, so he'd suffer right along with the woman he loved if only to spend a little more time with her.

The evenings were what he looked forward to the most. After a long day's work, they could spend some quiet time together without prying eyes or the frustration over the distance growing between Agatha and her son.

Most of the time they spent together was out in the clearing from their first date. Picnics didn't happen often, but they weren't necessary when he could settle back on a blanket in the meadow, hold her hand, and stare at the sky.

Zeke traced his thumb over her soft hand as they looked at the glittering sky. She shifted so her head could rest against his shoulder and sighed. "You know what's funny?" she asked.

"Hmm."

"I keep thinking about what's going to happen when the house is done."

He smiled. "You'll get your home back, and so will I."

She snickered. "That's not what I meant and you know it." She lifted herself up onto her elbow and gazed at him. Her eyes and skin glowed from the natural light of the moon, bright and angelic. "What are we going to tell people when they realize we're still seeing each other when we don't have to."

"What do you mean?"

"Like in town? Right now, we see each other every day to work on the house at least for a few hours. What happens when the house is done? I don't see you coming over for breakfast every morning."

His lips curled into a crooked smile. "Why not?"

"Don't be ridiculous. On top of that, we've been spending nearly every evening together as well. We're going to have to say something. I mean… what if it's time we stop hiding it?"

He lifted his hand and pushed it into her hair as he cupped the side of her face. "Are you sure?"

"Why not? We've been spending so much time together. We're about as close as a couple can get without being engaged or married." Her body stiffened, and she glanced away briefly. "What I'm trying to say is that I think Thomas has started to assume that something is going on that I'm not telling him, too. It's the way he looks at me. We're strangers. I think it would be a good idea to tell him that we're dating and just be done with it."

Zeke sat up. "I don't know if that would help matters much." He stared out at the dark tree line, resting his forearms on his raised knees.

She shifted beside him, scooting closer. "Why do you say that?"

"Because your relationship is already strained, and the reason is because he's keeping something from you. Do you really think he's going to be thrilled about you doing the same? What if he blames you for doing so just to get back at him?" It could happen. Zeke had considered this once he'd found out about Thomas's secret girlfriend in the city. On the other hand, it could go completely different. Confessing their relationship might make Thomas feel secure enough to confess his own.

Both had a chance of ending badly for Agatha and himself —a fact he wasn't ready to deal with at the moment.

"I never thought of that," Agatha said. "His hiding whatever it is has definitely created a wedge between us. I don't want to make it worse. But what else can I do? I can't just stand by and act like everything is okay. It's not."

"I didn't say it was." Zeke peeked at her, finding her staring at her hands. That disappointment tore at him. He was being the selfish one now. Keeping her from talking to her only family—now *that* was something she could break up with him over. His stomach knotted and churned with guilt. At this point, there was no way for him to come out on top, and he'd just have to accept it. It didn't matter that Agatha was the first woman he'd thought twice about in a romantic way. She needed to know, and he'd simply have to live with the outcome.

He took a deep breath and faced her, but she cut him off.

"You're right. I shouldn't tell him about us until he's ready to come clean about what's going on. I don't want to make this argument with him about our relationship, and if he were to use it against me, I'm not sure how we'd deal with it." Her forced smile didn't reach her eyes. In fact, the emotion there was the same as it had been for the last couple of weeks. "Besides, I like *this*—you and me. It's nice not having to share you with anyone yet."

"Yeah..." he said. "Me too."

ANOTHER WEEK PASSED, and the secret Zeke kept from Agatha was now messing with his sleep schedule. He had a hard time getting to sleep, and when he did, it wasn't restful. The only thing that kept him going was knowing he was protecting her in a way she might not realize she needed. If he'd learned anything from her, it was that she needed control just as much as he did.

Unearthing this secret would take that control away from her.

The cabinets were going in today. Drills and saws numbed his senses, and he was able to dive into his work because

Agatha had told him she was planning on heading to town for some paint swatches for the upstairs rooms.

Studs needed to be found and the cabinets anchored. They had slabs of marble for the countertops. Then it would be on to the tiling work. Everything was finally coming together, and his conversation with her regarding what would happen next came to the forefront of his mind.

Eventually everything would have to come out. Nothing could be secret forever—and he wasn't so sure he wanted to keep hiding how he felt about her anyway. It had been fun—made him feel young again—but it was time to be mature about all of this.

This evening he'd tell her exactly that. She would listen to logic. She'd be able to see that he'd been protecting her, and then she could clear the air with her son and everything would work out.

Still, his insides revolted. What if she didn't? There was still a real possibility of that happening, too.

"You wouldn't believe it, but I drove all the way to town and the paint shop was closed." Agatha dropped her purse down on a step ladder in the kitchen. "Thank you for letting me borrow your truck. Sorry I wasted the gas." Her focus swept through the kitchen and a smile flooded her face. "This looks great."

"What are you doing here?" Zeke charged through the kitchen and attempted to herd her into the living room, but she darted around him.

"I told you. The paint shop was closed so I just came back."

"But you said you were going to get some lunch and maybe pick out some hardware, too." She was back too soon. There was a lot more going on in the kitchen than had been as of late—a great deal more than possibly everything before this point except for the framing.

And suddenly, his nerves were shot. He could think of a thousand ways she might get hurt or worse just by being in this room. He thought he was worried about her finding out that he was keeping a secret from her, but in reality that was nothing.

Zeke would never forgive himself if Agatha got hurt.

When he stepped in front of her, blocking her from being able to get a better look at the work being done, she shot him a dark stare. "What are you doing, Zeke?"

"Nothing." His knee-jerk response did nothing to shift her focus from him.

"No." She wagged her finger toward him. "This. Whatever it is, you need to stop."

Shrugging, Zeke shook his head. "I don't know what you're talking about. I'm not doing—"

She let out a frustrated sigh. "You're trying to stop me from coming into my own kitchen."

He lifted his brows, ready to deny.

But hadn't he just decided they needed to be more mature about everything? There was nothing wrong with him trying to keep her safe. She should be willing to accept that. The drilling continued behind him as another cabinet was secured to the wall. Whoever was working on it climbed down the ladder, the steps creaking. Zeke set a firm gaze on the woman he loved. "Fine. I'm trying to keep you out of the kitchen—but it's just for today."

She scoffed.

"I mean it, Agatha. You don't need to be in here. You already picked out the cabinets and the layout. Don't you think hovering is a little overkill?"

Her mouth dropped open. "Overkill? This coming from the guy who wouldn't let his daughters date."

Those words hit below the belt. Zeke flinched but recovered just as quickly. "That's different. I was keeping my daughters safe like I'm trying to keep *you* safe."

Sean shot Zeke a strange look from where he stood beside the next cabinet he planned on putting in place. Thankfully he didn't say anything, but Zeke might have to have a talk with him before he headed home to Adeline.

"Safe? You can't be serious. There's nothing in here that would hurt me. Do you even hear yourself? You make it sound like women aren't capable of doing anything with power tools. That's so *backwards*."

"Well, I was raised right. Women shouldn't have to worry about this sort of stuff because…"

Her death glare made him reconsider where he was going with his next statement. She poked him in the chest, and he took a small step backward. "I can do just as much as you can. Just because I'm female doesn't mean I'm any less qualified."

"No, but the fact is that if one of those cabinets happened to fall on you, you'd be seriously hurt."

"So would *you*," she shot back. "Stop acting so ridiculous." She pushed past him, inadvertently bumping into the ladder where Sean stood with the drill. It teetered, causing Sean to lose his grip on the power tool he held in his hand so he could catch his balance.

Agatha gasped, her hands flying up as if to ward off anything that might hurt her. The idea was laughable. Either the drill or the full-grown man would definitely do some damage, and no amount of holding up her hands would stop it.

Zeke lunged forward and grabbed the drill mid-air. The bit cut into his hand before he got a firm grasp on it, drawing blood.

Agatha's wide eyes jumped to Zeke, then to Sean.

"You good?" Zeke muttered, holding out the drill.

Sean nodded. "You?"

He shook out his hand. "It's just a scratch. I'll be fine."

Agatha reached for his hand, turning it over. "You need to get that cleaned."

He jerked his hand away, finding it hard not to throw just how right he'd been in her face. "Now do you believe me?"

She still seemed intent on getting another look at his hand. "What?"

"That you shouldn't be in here today."

Agatha frowned at him. "You can't seriously be blaming me for what just happened."

"Can't I? I've been around the block before. Just because you think you can do something doesn't always mean you should. Because of your carelessness, you might have been the one to get hurt, and then what? I'm not going to let that happen on my watch. I want you off of the property."

"What?" Her voice rose an octave. "You can't kick me off my own property."

"Watch me," he said, holding out his hands at either side to block her from moving past him this time. Thankfully, she backed up rather than pushed forward. Once he got her to the door, he moved so he filled the whole thing. "Take my truck. Head back to the cabin. I'll take the ATV."

Her eyes seemed to drill into his as if telling him that he would regret doing this. Unfortunately for her, he'd had several years of practice being the bad guy. He didn't care if she was mad at him as long as he knew she was safe.

Agatha huffed, spinning quickly and heading straight for his truck. She got a few steps when they both realized she hadn't grabbed her purse. Before she could make an excuse to return inside to get it, Zeke snatched it up from where she'd placed it and held it out to her.

She tore it from his grasp and marched away without another word.

Zeke only flinched when she slammed the door shut. That was a lot easier than he'd expected. Maybe by the time he got done with the work he had to do today, she will have cooled off enough to listen to reason.

He returned to the kitchen, only to find Sean perched on

the top of the step ladder, a sly smirk on his lips. "Seems to me something's going on between the two of you."

"You'd be wrong. Get back to work."

"Nah. Something's going on. The Zeke I knew would have never let Agatha talk to him like that, let alone get close enough to cause even a hairline scratch. She's got you whipped." Sean's eyes widened and he stiffened. "Erm... sir."

"You best be keeping your theories to yourself, son. Gossiping doesn't look good on you."

22

Agatha

Who did Zeke think he was? He couldn't kick her out of her own home. She was the owner of the house, and as such, she had every right to be wherever she wanted to be, even if that meant right in the middle of all the action.

Hadn't she proven herself smart enough to be able to handle whatever the next project was? She'd seen the videos online. Women weren't put in boxes anymore. They could do hard things, and she'd spent most of her life trying to prove that very thing to others.

But apparently, Zeke wasn't prepared to accept that part of her life anymore. Something had shifted, and she had no idea what it was.

If Sean and some of the other men weren't on the premises, she might have stomped her foot and demanded he treat her like a partner and not some helpless damsel in distress. That was the furthest thing from how she viewed herself, and it was about time that Zeke believed it too.

The problem was, with the other men lingering, she couldn't say anything that might jeopardize where they were in their relationship. But oh, how she'd wanted to give him a little shove in the right direction.

Agatha returned to the cabin just like Zeke had requested, but she was far too amped up to do much more than pace around the building. At first, she counted the steps it took her to get around the whole thing. Then she moved on to how many times she'd walked the perimeter because the former got to be too much.

Her agitation continued to grow exponentially and all she wanted to do was call Zeke up and put him in his place. The drill issue wasn't her fault. Yes, she'd bumped into the ladder, but that was where her responsibilities ended.

She let out a groan, throwing her hands down at her sides as she picked up the pace. The second he got back to the cabin, she'd force him to make a promise that he'd never do something so embarrassing for the rest of their lives.

All this flurry of emotion had her wishing she wasn't still at odds with her son. It would have been nice to be able to vent about a man who wasn't willing to treat her like his equal.

It wasn't just Thomas who would have been a good sounding board. Shane was another person she'd opened up to a handful of times. The problem was she couldn't confide in him either because of his relationship with Zeke.

Why didn't she have any female friends?

Everyone she'd gotten close to since moving to Copper Creek were men. And they were all in the same social circle. So much for being independent.

Agatha refused to admit that her choice in friends had anything to do with her past, however. She'd fought to be released from a prison where she'd been placed. Hadn't she clawed herself out of an unfortunate circumstance where she didn't have any power? And now she found herself slipping back into a position where that would be taken away.

She knew Zeke had bad habits. He didn't prioritize equality. Going up against him would only continue to get harder. Agatha had to put her foot down if she wanted to ensure her future would remain the way she had grown accustomed to. That wasn't being selfish; that was advocating for herself.

The whole afternoon, she waited by the window, watching for Zeke to return to his campsite and leave his ATV where he usually did.

But as it got darker, she started to wonder if he was going to show up at all. Doubts continued to circulate in her mind. She cared for him deeply. She loved his company and spending time with him when he wasn't concerned for her safety.

Anyone else in her position would be patient. They'd make their concerns known, but only after everything cooled down. Perhaps it would be better for her to stay at one of the now-vacant motel rooms in town. She'd be able to clear her head and regroup. Ever since she returned home, she'd been on edge. Part of it had to do with Thomas, and the other was with Zeke.

A night alone would do her good.

Without giving it a second thought, she grabbed her purse and Zeke's keys for the truck she'd borrowed earlier and headed out. The farther she got from the cabin, the more at ease she became. Could it really be that simple? That this one act of taking control of her life had calmed her troubled heart?

Agatha pulled up to the first motel on the edge of town, and within ten minutes, she was all checked in. The place was built in the seventies, and it showed—from the carpet to the wallpaper. But she didn't mind one bit.

She dropped her purse on the small table and settled onto the edge of her bed. It was quiet—not the kind of quiet out in the woods where she had been staying—but still nice and peaceful. She didn't imagine that town was this peaceful when the rodeo folk had been around, but with them gone, she could see herself staying here had that been an option.

Laying back on the comforter, she trailed her hands across the fabric and closed her eyes. She focused on her breathing and before she knew it, she'd fallen asleep.

The next thing she knew, the light was coming in through the window. She stretched and sat up, feeling far more refreshed than she had any right to be.

Her head was clear. All her concerns from the night before seemed so far away and so... insignificant. She loved Zeke. They would be able to work out whatever life threw at them. She'd let things get away from her, and it was time to have a good old-fashioned conversation about expectations moving forward.

On that same note, she'd be having a discussion with her son. It was time to *really* take control of her life the way she always had.

Agatha retrieved her things and headed for the door, but the second she opened it, she froze. A man in a sheriff's hat and uniform stood right outside, his back to her. He turned to face her and stuck his thumbs into his belt loops. "Ms. Birch?"

"Yes? Is everything okay?" Immediately her concerns went to her son. "Is Thomas hurt? Did something happen?"

He waved a hand at her. "No, no. Everything's fine. Well... except..." He glanced over his shoulder toward Zeke's truck. "Did you come here using that truck?"

She shot a look toward the vehicle. "Yes. Is there a problem?"

"Seems Mr. Callahan has reported it missing."

Her mouth fell open. "He wouldn't."

"Sorry?"

Agatha cleared her throat and shook her head. "I was

borrowing his truck for errands yesterday. I had his permission..."

"Did you notify him of your plans to stay at the Sleep Inn Motel?"

"Well, no... but—"

"I'm sorry, ma'am. But I'm going to have to ask you to hand over the keys."

She shook her head. "This has to be a mistake. He wouldn't... we are..." When the sheriff lifted his radio to his mouth and glanced in her direction, she stopped. If Zeke reported the truck missing, he was either really mad at her, or he had assumed the truck had really been stolen.

"Were you saying something?" he asked.

Shaking her head, she jerked her purse around and dug through it. "This is all just a misunderstanding. I can call him, or I'm certain you have his phone number. Just tell him I have the truck." She pulled out her phone, finding there were several missed calls.

Her stomach dropped to the floor and her legs went weak. The device had been on silent all night. From the looks of it, not only had Zeke called her, but so had Thomas and Shane, as well as some unknown numbers.

She blinked rapidly, forcing herself to stay present. When she met the sheriff's gaze, she stammered, "Like I said, this is a misunderstanding. I needed to get away for the night and I didn't have my phone on. But if you must take the keys—"

He held up his hand as the radio crackled some nonsense she couldn't understand. But that could have been due to the ringing in her ears. Zeke was furious. She already knew it without even seeing him. Her son was likely in the same boat. Coming to the motel on a whim wasn't as great of an idea as she originally thought.

The sheriff offered her a polite smile. "I'm sorry, ma'am. I'm going to ask that you follow us in the vehicle to the sheriff's station."

"Am I under arrest?" Her voice squeaked and her palms went clammy.

"No, of course not. But we will have to take a statement, and it sounds like Mr. Callahan is there already in the process of filing a missing person's report."

"He's *what*? Oh, for heaven's sake. This can't be happening. I was gone one night. That was it." Agatha brushed past the officer and took a few steps toward the motel office before stopping. "I assume it will be okay if I check out before we leave?"

He nodded, seemingly confused, but over what, she couldn't figure out.

This was ridiculous. The whole situation was. Once upon a time she would have thought she was in complete control of her life, and somehow that truth had changed. Was it possible that this whole time she'd been fooling herself?

The whole way to the sheriff's station, she had to fight the temptation to turn the truck around and head back to the hunting cabin. No one was going to arrest her, and she could just drop off the truck and be done with it. She could let Zeke come to her and explain himself.

But instead, she played the well-behaved middle-aged woman who apparently had a great deal more sense than all of the men in her life.

The sheriff's station was mostly empty. The only vehicle she recognized was her son's. Great. He was here, too. Well, that just meant the conversations she'd been steeling herself for were going to happen sooner rather than later.

She got out of the truck and stormed toward the building's entrance. The second she got inside, she saw them. Her boyfriend and her son. Neither of them moved when they saw her. Agatha glared at them. Fine, if they wanted her to make the first move, she would.

"What in the world do you think you're doing?" she said, hands on her hips.

Thomas glanced toward Zeke, moderately surprised that she was talking to his boss instead of him. Zeke's expression remained schooled.

"I decide to stay in the city for one night and you two can't bother to give me twenty-four hours to show up again? I'm a grown woman, not a child."

"Mom, to be fair, you took Mr. Callahan's truck without—"

She shot him a dark look. "Mr. Callahan let me borrow it yesterday." She shifted her gaze to the man in question. "My apologies if there was a time limit I wasn't aware of." Agatha dug the keys from her purse and shoved them into his hand. "There. You have your truck back."

"That's not what this is about, Agatha," Zeke said.

"Oh? Let me guess. I'm too vulnerable to spend one night on my own in town, just like I'm too vulnerable to oversee the work on *my* home."

Once again, Thomas glanced toward Zeke. He shook his head as if he needed to clear it. "You weren't where you were supposed to be. The truck was gone. And you weren't answering your phone. What did you expect us to think?" Thomas said.

"I expected you to give it a day. It's not like we live in a crime-riddled city. We moved out here to get away from all of that, or don't you remember? You said the city wasn't where you wanted to be. I moved out here for you."

Thomas flinched and looked away, that aloofness she'd grown to expect rearing its ugly head.

"The boy has a point. You could have at least left us a message or told someone where you were going to be."

"What do you care? You're just the guy who wants me to get out of his cabin," she snapped. Her patience was officially gone.

The threads of her logical side had all but frayed, and she could no longer see the light. This was what she'd been so anxious about. She craved her independence. She needed to know that people respected her and trusted her to take care of herself.

Zeke stiffened. His eyes clouded over with something dark, almost sinister. If she didn't know him like she did, she might have been worried.

Agatha had struck a chord. From the beginning she'd always wondered if Zeke simply wanted his sanctuary back. During the good times, those concerns were buried deep. Part of her knew she shouldn't have even unearthed them, but it was too late now.

"Mom!" Thomas's voice rose. "Mr. Callahan's been generous and you know it."

All at once, everything around her settled. The storm brewing within her, the reality of how she was behaving. None of it was appropriate.

She flushed, ducking her head so she didn't have to meet either one of their gazes. "You're right, Thomas. Zeke—Mr. Callahan, I'm sorry. Based on what I saw getting installed yesterday, I think it would be best if I moved out of the cabin and started living at the house again. I can go without an oven until it's delivered and stay in one of the guest rooms upstairs." Agatha peeked at her son. "I just need to pack up my things."

Thomas shot an uncertain look toward Zeke, then nodded. "I can drop you off, but I have to put in my shift and won't be able to drive you home until after."

"I can do it," Zeke said gruffly.

Before she could decline, Thomas cut in. "Thanks, Mr. Callahan. We owe you so much. Mom? Let's get going. I have to be at work in thirty minutes."

Agatha avoided looking directly at Zeke as she said, "Sorry again." She prayed their next encounter would go smoother, but if she were honest with herself, she knew better. There was still dust in the air that needed to settle before either one of them would be able to figure out what to do next.

23

———

Zeke

Zeke wouldn't know how to describe the fury that burned from every organ he had. It was more than just fury. It was terror. When he'd returned to the cabin to find it empty, his first thought had been that Agatha had gone for a walk to clear her head.

He'd spent a good thirty minutes stomping through the brush looking for any sign of her, only to remember that his truck was supposed to be at the cabin and there was no sign of that either.

But realizing the truck was missing only complicated matters even more. Agatha could be anywhere. What did she need with his truck? And that wasn't to say that she hadn't returned it to his house and then gone somewhere else.

Twelve painstaking hours this worry festered inside him, making him wonder if he'd ever see her again. There was a reason he kept those he loved close. There was less of a chance that any of them would get hurt.

Then Thomas showed up at the cabin, and that was when Zeke knew that something bad had happened. In his gut, he could sense that something was wrong.

Thankfully, Thomas only blamed himself for his mother's disappearance. He had already apologized several times for his mother taking the truck without permission and pleaded for Zeke not to press charges. He was overheard speaking to someone on the phone over concerns that his mother had gone off the deep end.

Reporting the vehicle stolen had been a last resort, one he wasn't proud of, but at least it got results. They found the truck a mere two hours after Zeke called it in at six this morning.

Now Zeke had to figure out what he was going to do when he saw her again. He probably shouldn't have offered to take her to her home, but thanks to his impulsivity, he couldn't back out now. Ever since their argument at her house, he'd been trying to come up with a good way to tell her that she simply needed to be more careful. But after the way she'd overreacted and taken off without a word, he'd lost his resolve to do that.

It wasn't common, but every so often Zeke came across someone who needed to be set straight. He just hadn't thought he'd have to do something similar with Agatha. Up until this morning, he'd been able to look past some of her more reckless behaviors.

So as he marched up to the cabin's front door, he felt himself dragging his feet. He didn't want to have the conversation he knew they needed to have. What he wanted was to pull her into his arms and tell her he forgave her. He wanted her to promise she'd be more careful—but that wasn't about to happen. Somehow, he knew that deep down. The look in Agatha's eyes yesterday made it clear she didn't think she'd done anything wrong.

He knocked on the door, then leaned his forearm against the edge of the jamb. Each second that ticked by contributed to his nerves. They would be adults about this, and as soon as they cleared the air, they'd figure out the next steps for their relationship.

She opened the door, swinging it inward with such force that the tendrils of her hair framing her face floated up and then down again. Agatha glanced up at him, then released the doorknob and retreated inside. "I'm almost ready."

"Agatha—"

"With all due respect, I really don't want a lecture from you right now, Zeke."

He snapped his mouth shut, then his eyes narrowed as he entered and shut the door behind him. "I'm not going to lecture you." At least he didn't think of it that way. "We can have a conversation about what happened though."

She huffed, then turned to continue putting a few things in a nearby box. "When you say conversation, you really mean you're going to tell me what I did that you didn't like and how I was wrong to do it."

"You're making me sound—"

"Controlling? Are you really surprised?" She kept her focus trained on her task and her voice remained tight. Then she sighed, dragged the back of her hand across her forehead and faced him with folded arms. "You don't have to tell me anything. You want me to say you were right and I was wrong? Well, I won't. Because the only thing I would have changed was calling an Uber instead of taking your truck. I should have known better than to assume that you would be okay with your girlfriend borrowing your truck."

"That's not what this is about and you know it," he growled, frustration growing.

"I get it. You're upset—"

That was the final straw. Agatha was clearly not seeing things from his side—not even a little bit. "Upset doesn't begin to cover it." At some point his hands had curled into fists. His jaw was tight, aching from how he spoke through gritted teeth. "Can't you even pretend to understand what your son and I went through when we couldn't contact you? For all we knew, you could have been lying in a ditch somewhere."

She huffed again. "I'm not some teenager who doesn't know how to handle herself. I guarantee that anyone who might have wanted to do me harm would have walked away worse for wear."

"That's not what this is about!" His voice raised a decibel and she stilled, her hardened expression softening.

"Do you know how many people die in car accidents in a year? And it's not due to the driver's own negligence, either. You left the house upset. Your driving could have very well been impaired. On top of that, when Thomas stopped by for dinner like he usually does and you weren't here..." Zeke shook his head, dropping his hands listlessly at his sides. "I've never seen a man so worried for someone. He thought he was the reason you left."

At least that seemed to get to her. Agatha's eyes brimmed with emotion and her nose pinked. For a moment he thought she might say something to indicate she felt some kind of remorse. But then her eyes hardened. She didn't look at him directly, and her voice lowered so quietly that he barely heard it. "The problem with both of you is that you can't seem to accept that I don't need a man in my life." She glanced at him briefly. "I'm still his *mother*, Zeke. I'm a long way off from needing him to care for me. *I'm* supposed to be the one to take care of him. That's my job." Her voice was laced with pain—something he knew he couldn't fix.

"I wasn't saying—"

"And *you*." She pointed at him, and he stiffened. "You stand there all high and mighty, acting like just because you have feelings for me and I have feelings for you that you can suddenly tell me what I can and can't do. I'm not one of your wayward daughters. I've lived my life on my terms up until this point, and I'm not going to let anyone change that. I *chose* you, Zeke. You didn't have to be a part of my life. I *let* it happen. And at this point, I'm not so sure I made the right decision."

Like a shotgun had gone off pointed directly at his heart, her words shattered him. "What are you saying?"

She just stared at him. Her shoulders lifted, then dropped, and she looked away. "Honestly? I don't know."

"That's a load of bull pucky. Deep down you know you wouldn't have said anything if you didn't have a plan. So spit it out, Agatha. Tell me what you want."

Her brows creased and she shifted, though her focus was now glued to the floor. "There's something I don't get. It's been something that has been bothering me for a while, and I can't put my finger on it."

Zeke waited. What else could he do? She was withdrawing from him, and anything he might say right now could cause her to pull away even more.

"Did you know that Thomas still hasn't told me why he lied? It's been weeks, and he won't let me bring it up. He says it's in the past and to drop it. He won't even admit that it was just him wanting to hang out with some friends."

Zeke didn't know what he'd expected her to bring up, but this wasn't it. Of course Thomas wouldn't tell her that he was spending time with friends. The kid wasn't willing to lie a second time. The woman in the city wasn't just a friend, and from what Zeke could tell, things had continued to get more serious. On more than one occasion, Thomas had volunteered to head to the city with the guys to pick up supplies they didn't have in town. It wasn't hard to put two and two together.

"You seem to think that's normal." Her soft voice pulled him back to the conversation.

"I don't have any opinion on the matter," he said.

"Don't."

He stiffened. "What?"

"Don't lie to me."

"I'm not lying."

She sighed. "Out of everyone I know, you are the one person who would have a strong opinion about their child keeping something from them. You expect me to believe that you would be okay with it were one of your daughters who decided to keep their whereabouts from you?"

He took in a deep breath, held it for a moment, then blew it out. "Not that it's any of your business, but Brielle snuck off to Vegas right out of high school and got married."

The shock on her face might have been humorous if it weren't for the current situation.

"It's taken me several years to accept that if I had known all those years ago that she'd done it, nothing would be different than it is today. She's an adult. I did my best to raise her—all of my daughters—and they have to live their lives the way they see fit."

This time Agatha let out a wry laugh. "And yet you can't offer me the same courtesy."

Zeke shook his head as he removed his hat and ran a hand through his hair. "I'm sorry, but is this about Thomas and his lying to you or about something I've done?"

"Both." Her shoulders drooped. The stiffness of her body left—replaced by something that could only be described as giving up. "I can't explain it, but I have this feeling that ever since the fire, everyone in my life has been putting me in this... box."

"No one is putting you in a box. Do you hear how ridiculous that sounds?"

Her gaze darkened. "I wouldn't expect you to see it. What do you call what happened yesterday? What's happened since the very beginning? All I've wanted to do is be involved as my home gets repaired. That's it. I know I can't do everything, and maybe it's one of my shortcomings, but I need to feel... competent. That's just part of who I am. And having you standing just a foot away telling me I'm incapable of doing any of it is just so... *exhausting*." She finally relaxed, her eyes sad. "I can't live my whole life fighting to maintain what is inherently my identity."

"No one is stopping you from doing anything."

"Is that what you think? Because when you told me to leave *my home,* that's exactly what you were doing. Whether you like it or not, you've turned this into something it should have never been. You're still just as controlling as your reputation made you out to be, and honestly, I'm tired of feeling like all you want to do is babysit me."

He wanted to tell her she was wrong—to fight against what he could sense was coming next. Everything he thought he could control was slipping through his fingers, too. And that was when everything started to make sense.

Zeke couldn't believe he hadn't seen it before this moment. They would never work. They were far too similar, and at this point she probably had the best idea. They needed to separate before they did any deeper damage.

"You're right." He cut her off before she could say anything that would further hurt him. "You're right about all of it. I'm never going to be able to step aside because, let's face it, that's just who I am. I'm set in my ways." The words tumbled from his lips even as his heart revolted. *You could change if you really wanted to,* it seemed to say, but he wasn't having any of it. The wounds inside him already ran deep. He'd lost too much in his life to risk losing another woman.

"That's not what—"

He held up his hand. "I was a fool for thinking I could change you, and as much as I hate to admit it, that's exactly what I was trying to do. I wanted to fit you in a little box, but you didn't belong there."

"Zeke, wait—" she stammered.

"No. I'm not going to force you to be something you're not. And I suppose I just want the same courtesy. It's best if we just part ways before either one of us gets really hurt. I'll take you to the house, and that will be that." He motioned toward a stack of cardboard boxes. "Do these need to get loaded up?"

She glanced toward the stack, but her eyes seemed glazed over. He'd finally got her to stop talking, but it did nothing to ease what he was feeling. He could almost feel his body revolting against what his head knew was the path he needed to take. His heart, stomach, every inch of him demanded that he take back what he'd said.

Fight for her, you idiot.

Zeke clamped his mouth shut, then without waiting for her to make a comment regarding the boxes, he picked up the first one. Once he reached the door, he stopped but didn't face her. "You have good instincts, Agatha. I wouldn't forgive myself if I didn't let you know that you are right about your son. You might find me controlling, but that's just the kettle calling the pot black. Thomas is worried about disappointing you. Perhaps level the playing field before you have that conversation with him."

24

———————

Agatha

Agatha felt utterly numb. This wasn't how things were supposed to go. She'd expected Zeke to be upset about her putting him in his place. She'd seen men put up defenses like the Great Wall of China over small insignificant things, but this wasn't that.

He'd blasted through that wall and tore everything down that they'd created.

Well, could you blame him? You practically told him that he was driving you crazy. Nobody wants to feel that way.

On top of this numb feeling, Agatha couldn't understand where everything had gone so terribly wrong with her son. They'd always had a great relationship.

At least she'd thought they had.

She stood in front of the window, watching Zeke's truck drive away. It didn't matter how hard she hugged herself; she couldn't shake the feeling that she'd done something so irreversibly wrong.

The problem was that she knew she'd needed to have a conversation with Zeke about what had happened. She needed to be heard. If she couldn't voice her concerns, then how were they ever going to make things work?

And how were they going to make things work if Zeke ran off and hid from their relationship after one big fight?

Agatha scowled, turning from the window if only to prevent herself from getting emotional. There were bigger problems that needed solving. She'd been alone this long. She could continue living this way until the day she died.

But the problem with her son needed to be resolved. She refused to lose her family over her own miserable flaws.

Her son would be off work in a few hours and she'd be able to sit him down and ask him what Zeke was talking about. Hopefully, that conversation would go over better than the one she'd had with Zeke.

AGATHA PLACED a TV dinner in front of Thomas on the coffee table and settled beside him on the couch. "I know it's not what I've been making when you had dinner with me at the cabin, but—"

"It's fine, Mom."

She tossed him a side-eyed stare. They hadn't really talked about the visit to the police station. Doing so would open a whole can of worms she wasn't sure she was ready to spill. As much as she wanted to corner him about his lie, she couldn't— not until she told him why she had Zeke's truck in the first place.

Agatha heaved a sigh as she placed her food tray on the table. "I think we need to talk."

"Yeah. You've been acting kinda weird lately." He shot a look at her, and a hint of a smile graced his handsome face. "You're not going through a midlife crisis or anything, are you?"

She gasped and gave him her best mom-stare. "Don't you even suggest such a thing."

"Well, you *did* steal a truck from my boss... so..." He put a bite of food in his mouth, but it didn't prevent him from raising his eyebrows at her. But then his features grew serious. "Why did you do it? You've never been impulsive like that before."

This was it. This was the moment she'd have to tell him that she'd been seeing his boss without him knowing it. At least if she told him first before he found out from someone else, she could pull Thomas to her side. What kind of man was willing to call the sheriff on his girlfriend, anyway?

She straightened in her seat and rolled her shoulders. "It's a long story. You sure you're up for it?"

Thomas shrugged. "It's better than not knowing."

Agatha gave him a pointed look, but he must not have noticed. She couldn't blame him if he ended up keeping everything from her. If she could get through this conversation and not have to reveal her secrets, she might have considered it. But she needed to be the example. Too many secrets were making her mind unravel. "I guess it started the night of the fire."

He glanced at her, not even a hint of surprise on his face. Perhaps he thought she'd gone off the deep end due to the traumatic experience. That would certainly track. How many people did strange things as a way to cope with a new reality?

"I met Mr. Callahan when he showed up on that horse and tried to save me from a burning building even though I wasn't inside." She looked away. The next bit was going to be hard to explain away. How could she keep her growing feelings a secret when she'd had no problems sharing everything up until this point? "I fully expected him to be some brute who bossed people around because he had the money and the power to do so. But I was wrong."

Thomas had stopped taking bites of his food and his tray was now beside hers, both of them getting cold.

"Little by little I got to know him better. I realized that there was more to Zeke than meets the eye. He was compassionate. He loves his family above all else. But most of all, he was generous—to someone who was nothing more than a complete stranger." She took a long, unsteady breath. "I found myself developing feelings for him." Even though she whispered it, she felt like she'd screamed it from the rooftops.

And she might as well have done that very thing for the look of shock on her son's face.

She just needed to cut to the chase. Letting this conversation drag out like this wasn't good for either of them. "I was dating him, Thomas. I didn't want to tell you because I didn't know what the folks in town might say. I didn't want you to get the wrong idea about him—or me."

"You were dating... my *boss*?"

She'd expected him to get angry. But all she heard was disbelief, something that threw her off guard momentarily. "We were involved, but we aren't anymore. I think we realized that we just won't work. We're too similar."

Thomas settled back on the couch. "I don't believe it."

Agatha placed her hand on his knee. "I'm so sorry I didn't tell you. I didn't want to make things complicated at work. Or between you and Zeke. I just..." What could she say that wouldn't sound selfish? She wanted to have some fun? Zeke made her feel things she hadn't felt in a long time? Any answer she ran through her head did just that. None of her decisions in the recent weeks indicated she had any consideration as to how they would affect her son.

He huffed. "Well, this actually makes a lot more sense."

She shot a glance at Thomas, finding him staring at her. There was no malice, but there was also zero happiness in his gaze.

"I thought something weird was going on between you and Zeke, but my mind never went... *that far*." He stood abruptly. "How long have the two of you been involved? Is that why..." Thomas faced her, his arms folded. "How long?"

"Not more than a couple months. I'm sorry I didn't tell you."

"I'm not upset."

"Really? I'd understand if you were."

"Well, I'm not." He sighed but didn't say anything else. The silence that continued to grow between them wore on her.

"Well, it doesn't matter anyway. We cut everything off. It was really for the best." She reached for her food, if only to keep her hands busy. Confessing her secrets was only part of the reason they needed to have this conversation. "You're probably wondering why I brought this up in the first place."

"Not really."

She shot him a surprised look.

"I can't believe he called the cops on you! Seriously, what kind of guy does that? You were dating him, and he didn't like that you borrowed his truck?"

Agatha bit back a smile. "You've got a decent point there."

Thomas laughed. "I mean, I guess I can understand why he was so worried now, but I would have never told the sheriff to hunt you down."

They ate in amicable silence for a few moments, and then she finally tossed him a smile. "You know, I really am sorry about keeping this from you."

He shrugged. "It's fine."

Strange. She was certain he would have been more upset. If he had been younger, she knew without a doubt that he would have held it against her. But something told her that his easy-going nature about this didn't have as much to do with maturity as she would like to think.

"I was wondering if you were up for telling me where you really were that one night..."

It wasn't hard to see she'd hit a nerve with that statement. He frowned and his jaw tightened. "I told you it didn't matter."

"You're wrong."

"No, I'm not. I can decide what is important to share and what isn't. We're both adults, and I'm not ready to talk about it."

"So, Zeke was right."

He stiffened further, freezing so much that he appeared to look more like a statue than a real human. "Zeke talked to you about me?"

"All he said was that you were keeping something from me because you didn't want to disappoint me."

Thomas released a pent-up sigh that resembled a groan. "If I were you, I wouldn't put much stock in what he might have said."

"Zeke might have a lot of flaws that I didn't like, but he never lied to me."

"I didn't say he lied, but is it possible he was making you look in one direction when you should have been looking in another?" Thomas stood again. "I don't want to talk about this. I'm not interested in spilling what's going on with me. That's not to say that it's never going to happen, but can we just not talk about it?" All it would take was for her son to take a dozen steps in one direction and he'd be able to escape.

But ultimately, it came down to one unalienable truth.

Agatha couldn't control Thomas any more than Zeke could control her. She'd gone from having two close relationships with the two men in her life that meant the most to her... to having neither.

She could feel a shell wrapping around her, closing her off from the outside world as if it were tangible and she could touch it. Words of assurance stuck in her throat, the disappointment like a sticky glue that prevented any movement. She nodded, fighting back emotion.

Somehow, she'd known this was going to happen eventually. She'd lose the close relationship she'd had with her son. She just didn't want to accept just how much it stung.

Agatha gathered her TV tray and stood as well. Thomas moved away from her an inch, and she offered him a sad smile. "You're far too old for me to tell you what to do, and even if you were still a teenager, I don't think anything I could have said would be enough to sway you in one direction over the other. I value my own freedom too much to force you to lose what you have. If you don't want to talk about it, then don't."

She moved past him, hating how it felt like the end of an era. This was the natural way of things. She should have just been thrilled their closeness lasted this long. At least soon, he'd move back home until the day came when he found some girl who would make him happy.

"Mom?"

She stopped and faced him.

"I did want to talk to you about something."

Hope flared to life within her. Their relationship was so disjointed. Here was a chance for her to heal whatever rift had been torn between them.

"I don't think I'm going to move back in with you."

Agatha nearly dropped the TV dinner she held. "What?"

He forced a smile, but it looked more sad than anything else. "I'm an adult. I've lived at home long enough. And I've realized I like being on my own. It's nice to be in the wrangler's bunkhouse while I'm working."

"So you're not moving back here... but this place is your home."

Thomas shook his head. "It's your home, Mom. You bought this place when I got the job. You moved out here to stay close to me when you could have stayed in the city. It's like you upended your life just because I made some small changes in mine. I don't want you to base your whole life and your decisions on me."

What was that supposed to mean? Was he actually accusing her of making decisions based solely on his career choices? "That's not true, Thomas. Yes, I moved out here to be closer to you, but I didn't have to. I thought you wanted me to."

He sighed and his gaze dipped to the floor. "Sometimes I wonder if things would be better if you had decided to stay where you were. It's hard for a bird to leave the nest when his mother keeps bringing it to him."

She officially felt sick to her stomach. Thomas felt smothered. No, he hadn't said it in so many words, but that was exactly how he felt, and she could see it as clearly as the nose on his face. He wanted to put some distance between them.

Agatha swallowed hard and nodded again. "I understand," she rasped. "You need room to spread your wings and I haven't really let you have that. I'll try to be more mindful of that." She couldn't bear to hear his response. She had to get out of that living room before he said something that really made her want to bawl her eyes out.

The TV dinner was tossed into the garbage, and she hurried toward the stairs. Her breathing came in short puffs. As many times as she'd told Zeke that she wanted independence, she had to admit one very real fact.

She hadn't been truly alone her entire life. First, she was with her family. Then her ex-husband. Then Thomas. Living in the cabin had been her first real experience of being on her own, and even then, she wasn't; Zeke had been nearby.

Her heart fluttered madly. What if it was all talk? What if she couldn't handle being alone any more than Zeke could handle keeping his controlling opinions out of anyone else's business?

The fluttering grew harder and more erratic, so much so

that she had to clutch at her chest and focus on her breathing. She'd be fine. She was just tired. Everything would work out the way it was meant to and she'd get back to work just like she knew she could.

Only now, she wasn't so sure.

25

Zeke

Zeke glared into his coffee. Thankfully none of his daughters were in the house this morning when he got up. He should have been happily moved into the cabin again, but even that place felt lonely as could be.

He just couldn't win.

Ever since his daughters started pairing up with their men, Zeke had felt at odds with himself. Nothing felt right anymore. He couldn't escape into his work because several of his family worked for him. He couldn't hide away at home due to how quiet it had become. And now he couldn't stand the kind of quiet that was taking place at the cabin.

In hindsight, Zeke had probably gone a little overboard in trying to keep Agatha safe—safe from herself, from her son, and from outside forces that could harm her. And all of that work was for nothing.

She couldn't appreciate what he'd done for her, and if that was the case, then he didn't need to be part of her life.

So why did he feel so absolutely desolate now?

She was just his neighbor. Perhaps in a different lifetime, she could be something else—something more.

"That coffee of yours must contain the secrets to the universe... or something similar."

Before he even looked up, he knew who had walked into the room. The last of his daughters to find a mate, the one who he'd thought he might not survive. "Good morning, Brielle. Now what reason would you have to be here this early in the morning?" He lifted his gaze to his daughter, who stood in the doorway.

She crossed her arms and her coy smile remained on her face. "It's just you and me now. So you can tell me who this woman is that you like so much."

"There's no one." Zeke sighed.

"You can't keep telling me that. I know there's someone because I'm the only one who set you up with someone, and she said you haven't called her. How do you think that makes me look?" Her voice was light, making it clear that she wasn't really upset that he hadn't called Charlotte. But he could tell, based on the look that filled her face, that she didn't like being left in the dark. She wanted details.

Zeke got to his feet, his coffee unfinished and now cold. "There was someone. Now there isn't. So there's nothing to tell. Charlotte isn't my type, and perhaps neither is this other woman. As far as I can tell, I'm not meant to find anyone to live the rest of my life with."

He didn't want to meet her gaze. If he had it his way, he would have slipped out of the kitchen and headed out to the barn so he could occupy his thoughts with other things. Except that was not what fate had in mind for him.

Brielle blocked his path. This time the smug expression was missing. She actually looked upset. Her brows were creased and turned upward in the middle. If he wasn't mistaken, she looked like she was about to cry.

But that wasn't Brielle's way. She reached out and touched his forearm. "What happened?"

Zeke shrugged. "Nothing. That's what I'm saying. It was short. It didn't mean anything. It's over, and that's that."

"Based on what you just said, I can tell this is hurting you more than you'd like to admit."

He sighed. "Look, sweetie. I can appreciate that you're worried about me. I can even understand the part of you that wants to toy with me a little bit and set me up on dates."

"Dad, that's not what—"

"It's fine. It's nothing less than I deserve."

"But Dad—"

Zeke held up a hand and waved her off. "Don't you worry about it. I'll be fine. I've been alone this long. It's nothing I can't handle." He forced a smile. "Besides. My family has already doubled, right? I don't need anyone else to make my life fulfilling." He pulled her in for a hug and then stepped around her.

Brielle's voice could be heard calling out to him, but he ignored it. He'd made his decision, and when that happened, he didn't go back on it. His gut instincts were usually right on the money.

When it came to Agatha, they were both better off without each other. She was probably already feeling better about her situation. She had her house back—well, for the most part— and she didn't have him butting into her life in ways that she couldn't stand.

That was probably the best thing he could do for her—the best housewarming gift there was.

Zeke headed out to the barn, going through the motions of what used to be his day-to-day. By the time the horse was saddled and he was heading out of the barn, he couldn't remember doing any of it. His brain was in such a fog.

His thoughts continued going to the same place.

What was Agatha doing today? They didn't have any house renovations planned since they were waiting on a delivery. He almost wanted to head over there and take a look at the work they'd completed just for an excuse to see her. But the need to rush to complete the project was nonexistent now.

Zeke shook his head. He needed to remain strong. No weakness.

At least by now, Agatha had probably figured things out with her son. Zeke could count that as one of his good deeds. Their strained relationship would be fixed, and he wouldn't have to feel so torn up over the secret he kept.

He led his horse along a trail, finding himself heading in the direction of his cabin.

No, not his cabin.

Toward the neighbor's property.

Immediately, he pulled up on the reins and stopped. What was wrong with him that he couldn't even keep the promise he'd made to himself? He glared at the trail that would take him to the place where he both wanted and didn't want to go. His heart and his head battled against one another. What would be so bad about visiting her?

She'd probably yell at him and tell him to leave her property.

Or she'd get upset that he'd kept such a secret from her. Admittedly, he should have told her the second he knew why Thomas was lying about his overtime. At least then, one issue would have been resolved by now.

But what if she admitted she was wrong and she wanted him in her life? The glimmer of hope that lit in his chest just wasn't enough to make him follow that path. He yanked on the reins and turned around but then nearly had a heart attack. Thomas stood beside a horse, holding its reins and staring up at him.

His expression was guarded. He didn't look upset exactly, but he definitely didn't look pleased.

Zeke stifled a groan. What had he done in another life to deserve all of this meddling from people who were half his age?

"Mr. Callahan, can I have a word with you?" From his position on the ground, Thomas should have looked intimidated. At least, that was what most folks felt when they came up against Zeke.

But not Thomas. If anything, he seemed to have grown some confidence in the last twenty-four hours.

Zeke crossed his arms, then leaned over the saddle horn, his head tilted slightly to the side. "What can I do for you, son?"

There was a flicker—an irritation—in Thomas's eyes that gave Zeke a small degree of pleasure. His eyes tightened, as did his jawline. But then he lifted his chin and his eyes narrowed. "I seem to recall a conversation with you where you mentioned it wasn't your place to tell my mother about something you discovered about me."

"And I didn't."

"Not in so many words, no. But you did tell her that I was keeping something from her."

Zeke studied this young man before him. He couldn't get a read on him. Had everything gone smoothly? Had Thomas ripped off the Band-aid and told his mother what he'd been holding back? There was still a chance it all worked out.

Or had it exploded, causing Agatha to be in more pain than she should have been? His heart burst with concern and an undeniable desire to turn right back down this path so he could find her and tell her that everything would be okay. He'd gone through his own issues with his children. They'd had their share of struggles, but in the end things had worked out.

"Well? Do you have anything to say for yourself?"

Zeke didn't move. He continued watching Thomas, hoping he'd get at least some indication of how things had worked out with his mother. Then his eyes narrowed and he straightened. "You'd let your deception go on long enough. It was time for your mother to find out about—"

"That was up to me to decide," Thomas cut in. "With all due respect, my personal relationship with my mother is none of your business. What I choose to tell her or not tell her is on me. And if we end up having an argument about it, that's on me, too."

"With all due respect, you have no idea what you're talking about." Zeke knew he shouldn't have said it the second the words escaped his throat. But once they were out, there was no taking them back. "You're young. You don't have the same kind of understanding about the world as I do. So let me give you a free lesson on how your relationship with your mother should be."

"Excuse me—"

Zeke held up a hand, and his voice hardened. "You are all your mother has in this world. She's got no one else. You are everything to her. And while I don't exactly agree with how you two have chosen to maintain said relationship, I can't say that the alternative has been much better. She deserves more from you."

Thomas opened his mouth again, but Zeke wasn't about to let him get a word in edgewise. "I've got at least thirty years on you, boy. Listen when I tell you that there is no reason to keep secrets from your mother like you've been doing. She deserves to know what's going on in your life and how it will affect not only you but her as well. And I'm not saying that telling her should change the decisions you're making, but perhaps you should be asking yourself why you didn't want to tell her in the first place."

"What don't you understand about the fact that I'm an adult and I get to decide what I'm going to tell my mother and what I don't?"

Zeke let out a dry chuckle as something dawned on him. "You didn't tell her, did you?"

Thomas folded his arms. "No, I didn't."

"And why not?"

"Because what good would it do? She doesn't need to know about a relationship I've started with someone when knowing would only hurt her."

"And why would it hurt her?"

"Because if it works out, then her moving out to Copper Creek was for nothing. She'd pick up and follow me again." His tone had turned exasperated. He dropped his arms to his sides and shook his head. "I love it here, and I can tell she loves it here too. But if I move, I know she's going to follow me and end up missing this place more than she will ever admit." Thomas peered up at Zeke and then glanced away. "And if it didn't work out and I ended up finding my way somewhere else, then she would just keep with the status quo. I have to figure out my life now. It's not that I don't want her to be a part of it. I just want her to be okay with wherever I end up. And I want her to be happy wherever she wants to be, even if that isn't in the same place as me."

Zeke stiffened. This was a side of things he hadn't considered. Thomas was trying to protect his mother in a similar way as Zeke had been. They were practically one and the same.

He bit back a smile. Agatha would hate this even more if she knew about it. But it wasn't his problem anymore. And perhaps it never was. Agatha was her own person, and she deserved to make her own decisions. "If your mother follows you from city to city, then that's her choice, and it's because she loves you. She's as much an adult as you are, and she can upend her life whenever she wants. But maybe you could let her know some of these things, then you wouldn't feel bad about it if she did decide to follow you."

Zeke waited for Thomas to argue—to make this all about him. But he didn't.

"And if you think that you're a disappointment for chasing your dreams, you couldn't be more wrong. You're her son. You're going to make mistakes, but as long as you end up happy, that's all she's going to want for you." The irony of Zeke's statement wasn't lost on him. He'd been on the other side of things. He'd been controlling and hard to live with. He'd set several rules for his daughters that didn't give them opportunities to grow. And how had that worked out for him?

On more than one occasion, his daughters had kept certain truths from him. He'd had to scramble to make things right. And now he didn't feel comfortable in his own home.

He shifted in his saddle, disliking how quiet Thomas had become, but for reasons he was only beginning to scratch the surface of. Thomas was no different than Zeke. He was just better at hiding it. "Believe me when I tell you that holding anything back from her is only going to make things worse. She deserves honesty. That woman raised you on her own. Don't you think, at the very least, she deserves to be let in on what's happening in your life?"

Thomas glanced up at Zeke once more. He worked his jaw back and forth for a moment, then nodded. "Yeah. I guess you're right."

A win. It was nice to be on the right side of things for once. Not only that, but he'd found himself in the position where he had finally done something that would actually help Agatha. She might not approve that he'd had to have a conversation with her son to do it, but at least he wasn't being the controlling person she thought him to be.

Advice. That was all.

Zeke smiled grimly at the young man. "Good. Now I just have one more thing to say. If you find yourself planning a move or a career change, please do us the courtesy of giving us your two weeks. I know my daughter would appreciate the heads-up before she has to find a replacement."

Thomas nodded again. He clicked his tongue, then pulled on the lead rope to turn his horse around. Then he stopped. Without facing Zeke, he said, "My mom misses you. I don't know what happened between the two of you, but I think she's regretting how it ended."

He started walking again, and when he was far enough away that he wouldn't hear, Zeke said quietly, "That makes two of us."

26

———

Agatha

Agatha threw herself into her work at Shane's. With most of the house renovations complete, she didn't have the motivation to finish the little details. She would like to blame it on getting tired of the same old thing, but she knew better.

Any time Agatha headed past the laundry room, she thought about the times Zeke yanked her inside to steal a kiss. When she walked past the living room and saw the photo album, she only saw Zeke's sweet attempts at soothing her when her house had been in shambles. There were memories everywhere she looked.

So instead of staying at home, she found every excuse to get out of her house. And now she was second-guessing herself more than she ever had in her life. Between her argument with Zeke and the conversation she had with Thomas, she wasn't sure about much of anything.

The only thing that made sense was her job.

So that was the one place she could find solace. Thankfully, Shane didn't seem to notice just how much more time she'd been spending at the country club rather than doing her work remotely.

Agatha sat at a booth near the entrance with her computer and let the world fall away. It was just her and the business Shane had created. If she were honest with herself, she'd say that this was the easiest job in the world. Shane already had a great grasp on his image and how he wanted the world to see him. There was so much charitable work he did on a quarterly basis that she didn't have to do much to help him keep up a positive image.

The only mess she'd had to clean up recently was the one with his cousin, and that was just to smooth over some ruffled edges.

She sat back and stared at her screen, wondering if there was something more she could do for him that she hadn't thought of. He didn't want to expand his business nationwide. Between the equine therapy for disabled children and military veterans and running the country club, he was busy enough as it was. The longer she sat here, the more she realized that she simply didn't have much of a purpose anymore.

Agatha settled back in her seat and stared at the screen.

That was it, then. She wasn't really needed as a mother. Her son was grown and wanting to put some distance between them. While she was paid well, she wasn't needed as much at her job. She didn't have someone to come home to.

The last few weeks where she'd been able to prepare meals for Zeke had been some of the most fulfilling of her life. What did that say about her that she depended on someone else to feel accomplished?

Had it been that way her entire life?

The ache in her chest from the loss of Zeke seemed to

spread to the rest of her body, making her feel hollow. She had thought she knew who she was and what she wanted.

She had thought wrong.

Someone slipped into the booth across from her and offered her a smile. "You're Ms. Birch, right?"

Agatha nodded. The woman was familiar. But that didn't mean much because everyone in town looked familiar. She could be anyone. "And you are?"

"Oh, I'm sorry. I'm Grace. My husband, Riley, and I work with the veterans here."

"Right. Of course. That's why you're so familiar." She squinted, then tilted her head. "Riley... I feel like I've met him."

Grace smiled warmly. "He's been helping my dad with your house."

Agatha could have slapped her forehead with her palm in that moment. Grace was one of Zeke's daughters, and Riley was his son-in-law. Geez. Was everyone around here related to the man? It was like Zeke truly was Copper Creek royalty. "Well, thank you so much for lending me your husband. The house is turning out better than I could have hoped."

"You're most welcome. That's what we do here." Grace stared at Agatha with a shrewd sort of expression. It was like she was expecting Agatha to say something more.

Unnerved, Agatha glanced away. "This town is pretty great," Agatha said.

They sat there for a few moments before Agatha couldn't take it any longer. "I'm sorry, dear. Was there something you needed?"

Grace shook her head. "Nope. I just wanted to come meet you. That's all."

That's when the realization hit her. Grace wasn't coming just to meet her. She wanted to meet the person who had broken her father's heart. This little get-together could mean so many different things.

Agatha leaned forward, prompted by something she couldn't understand. "I don't know what your father has told you, but—"

"My father hasn't told me anything," Grace stopped her, but her smile remained. "I figured it out on my own."

What exactly had she figured out? Was this about the relationship? The breakup? The fact that Agatha had made the biggest mistake of her life when she'd let Zeke walk away from her? Any one of those could be an answer to her question.

Grace reached across the table and took Agatha's hand in hers, gave it a small squeeze, then pulled away. "I can tell you make my dad happy. And I wanted to come meet the person who had finally brought some light back into his eyes."

A rock sunk to the bottom of Agatha's stomach, settling like a stone at the bottom of the dark ocean. It made her nauseous to realize what Grace's words meant.

She didn't know her father had broken things off between them.

Agatha shook her head. "I'm sorry. I don't know what you're talking about."

She laughed. "I might be the youngest in my family, but I've been doing this a long time. I can tell when something is going on, and it's not just what I saw with my father. It's what I'm seeing with you right now."

"And what is that?" Agatha had meant for her voice to sound strong and firm, but it came out as more of a quiet squeak.

"You've been dating my dad," she said triumphantly as she leaned back in her seat. "And for whatever reason, the two of you are trying to keep it under wraps."

Agatha shook her head. "You're mistaken—"

"The thing is, I get it. I can appreciate that you need to test things out before you tell the world about it. That's just the way it is sometimes. There are good reasons and bad ones." Grace's smile shifted to something different and her eyes got a far-off look in them. "But in the end, it comes out either way. It's for the best, really. Because then you can get the support of the people who love you. Sometimes we get in our own way, you know? And we make choices that end up hurting ourselves more than we realize."

"Wait... did he tell you?"

Confusion flickered across her features. "I told you, he didn't say anything about you. But that statement alone confirms my suspicions."

"No, I mean..." Emotion filled Agatha's throat. She had been caught, and now she had to admit to a truth she was quickly realizing wasn't something she wanted. "Yes, okay, we were *involved*. But that's changed."

"*Changed*?"

Agatha sighed, then pinched the bridge of her nose—anything to avoid having to look directly at the daughter of the man she'd developed feelings for. "We decided to break it off. It simply wasn't going to work between us."

"Why?"

Why. Agatha nearly laughed, but only because it would keep her from getting emotional. "Because we're just too similar and set in our ways. Neither one of us seems willing to change. And as I'm sure you're well aware," Agatha said, finally meeting Grace's gaze, "relationships require quite a bit of compromise. It just wouldn't work out, so we parted ways before we got too attached. It was for the best."

Grace shook her head. "You can't possibly believe that."

"Actually, I do."

"Then maybe you should reconsider things."

"I beg your pardon?"

Grace inched closer to Agatha, then rested her folded arms on the tabletop. "Yes, it's true people say that it's harder to change the older you get. But that's not a hard and fast rule. It's

like that old saying, 'You can't teach an old dog new tricks'—
except you can. The dog just has to be motivated."

Agatha pressed her lips into a thin line, trying not to be
offended at the fact that this young woman had just compared
her to a four-legged animal.

"Well, I think love is one of the best motivators. And if you
and my dad truly care about each other, then you would agree
that there is something both of you could do to make those
compromises you're so interested in."

"It's not that easy—"

"Isn't it, though? If you love someone, you're going to do
whatever it takes to make them happy. You'll do whatever it
takes to make it work, because you know that without them
in your life, you don't have anything." There was a deep
crease between Grace's eyes as she finished her speech. "If I
have learned anything, it's that there's more to life than
getting what you want, especially if that means that the
person you're making the sacrifice for is the person you care
about most."

Her words were like a bell tolling at the end of the day.
There was a resounding finality to them that made Agatha
wonder why she hadn't been able to see any of this before. And
yet she couldn't just drop it. "Let me ask you something, then.
What if the sacrifice you're speaking of requires one to walk
away from the person they love or risk making them miserable
for the rest of their life?"

Grace laughed. "You really *are* a lot like my dad. The analyt-
ical therapist in me would tell you that if you are honestly
unhappy in a relationship and you can't make things work no
matter what you try, then you ought to walk away with no
regrets." She tilted her head and offered a small, encouraging
smile. "But the stubborn Callahan blood in me would have me
tell you that love is hard work, but it will reap the best rewards.
You can't have the good without the bad. There will be good

days and bad days. There is only one question you have to ask yourself in this situation."

"And what is that?"

Grace beamed. "Do you really think you could live the rest of your life without him?"

"That's not a fair question. We barely just started our relationship."

"It's totally fair and even better, it's simple. Did you know that most people will figure out if they want to spend the rest of their life with someone after only three months? Some take as long as six months, but that's all it really takes. You've known my dad for three months. What do you think? Is he marriage material?"

"Well, of course he is. He's a good man with a generous heart, and he's clearly raised some wonderful children. But it's not just about whether or not he's marriage material. It's about—"

"It's about whether or not you want him in your life. Does he make you laugh? Does he make you feel like you're the only person in the world?"

Before Zeke, there was no one who showed a degree of interest in her—at least none that she knew of. He was the man who had made her feel again.

"See? I can tell just by the way you sorta disappeared just then."

Agatha's vision focused on Grace again.

"And guess what," Grace continued. "My dad feels the same way."

"You don't know that."

"I know a great deal more than you might realize. I pay attention to things like this. So, if you've already broken it off with him, he's got to be pretty miserable. If I were you, I'd call him and tell him that you made a mistake and you want to make things work."

The heart in her chest thrummed with the possibility of what lay before her, and then it faltered. "But your father was the one who ended it. I can't just go up to him and tell him he was wrong." She could feel her face filling with heat, hating the fact that Zeke had hit the nail on the head regarding their relationship. They were older, and they were set in their ways. And he hadn't requested that they find common ground. He'd just pushed her away.

"Why not?"

Agatha jumped, recalling what she'd asked. "Because that's just not how it's done. Also, he had valid reasons."

Grace laughed again. She was doing that a lot, and while it was a sweet sound, Agatha couldn't help but feel like she was the source of the amusement. "Things have changed since you were younger. If you want to mend a relationship with a guy, then do it. What is that saying? If you want something done right, then you have to do it yourself."

She made an excellent point. Agatha had always been the type of person that rolled up her sleeves and fixed what needed to be done. Why would this be any different?

The young woman in front of her got to her feet and pushed her hands into her pockets. "Ultimately, you're gonna do what you're gonna do. Don't let my words change your opinion on the matter." As she walked past, she touched Agatha's shoulder briefly, then stopped. "But if you decide to take matters into your own hands, I'd suggest showing my dad that you're not going to let him make all the decisions. He doesn't get to dictate what your relationship is any more than you do. It's like you said. There has to be compromises."

Agatha turned around to watch Grace wander off, not sure whether to be amazed or simply stunned that Grace had been so spot-on when it came to Agatha's relationship with Zeke.

Zeke had spent his whole life getting exactly what he wanted. Only recently, he'd made the choice to let his daughters have free rein. Well, he'd just met the one person who was willing to put him in his place and help him see that they needed to work together if they wanted to be happy.

She snapped her computer shut and gathered her belongings. If she was going to make a statement, it had better be one that left him speechless. Otherwise, what was the point?

27

Zeke

Regrets were not something Zeke experienced often. He'd managed to live his life making decisions he knew would be best for him or his family.

Right now, the regret he had over losing Agatha was something new. It hurt him in a way he hadn't expected. The more time that passed, the less he felt like himself, which made no sense at all.

On top of that, he knew the regret he had was due to his own selfish actions. Agatha would find happiness. Even if she was upset right now, she'd be glad to be free of him, which was why he'd decided to keep his distance between them.

What was hurting now would only last for a moment and then she'd get over it. She'd find something—or someone—she was passionate about, and then she'd go on living her life to the fullest. Zeke could be happy for her. At least that was what he kept telling himself as he yanked the pitchfork from the side of the hunting cabin and headed toward the small shed where he kept most of his supplies.

It had been two weeks since he'd last seen Agatha. He only went to her place when he knew she wouldn't be there and to help the others with the finishing touches. Now that the renovations were complete, he didn't have any reason to head in that direction ever again. Thomas kept his distance and so did his daughters. He probably had Brielle to thank for that, but then again, Grace might have had something to do with it. That girl had always had a knack for people-watching.

Everything was finally starting to feel normal again—better even. He was connecting with his daughters again in a way he hadn't since before Adeline married Sean. And now he felt strong enough to head back to the cabin to clean it up. No more retreating to the woods to hide from a life he should have been grateful to have in the first place.

Zeke trudged toward the shed and pulled open the door. He hung the pitchfork on the hook, then exited. Everything that needed to be taken care of outside of the cabin had been. Now, he needed to go inside and take stock of what needed to be done there.

He hadn't stepped foot inside the cabin since he'd helped Agatha move out. It wasn't something he felt he was strong enough to do. Something told him that her scent would have lingered and even getting a whiff of her perfume would have been too much for him.

A sigh was expelled from his lips as he stopped in front of the cabin's front door. Brielle and Wade had asked to use the cabin so they could have a little getaway from the chaos that was Wade's family. Zeke couldn't blame them. They'd been married for a little while now, and they didn't get much time to themselves.

Besides, if he let Brielle stay at the cabin, then she wouldn't be tossing him those knowing looks she seemed to have perfected when she paid him a visit. He dug into his pocket to retrieve his keys, then stepped forward to unlock the door, but it swung inward without him touching it.

He jumped backward a step as he came face-to-face with Agatha. His first instinct was to spin around in search of any signs that he might have missed. She'd been here this whole time while he cleaned up the shed and the exterior of the property, and yet she hadn't come out to tell him as much?

There were no signs, of course. For if there had been, he would have left.

Okay, he might not have left. There was a possibility that he would have mustered the courage to knock on the door and ask her what she thought she was doing at his cabin when she'd insisted on leaving.

Now he would never know what might have happened because he was standing in front of her and wondering what he should say.

I should tell her I miss her. No, she wouldn't believe him. If he missed her so much, he would have done something about it.

Tell her the biggest mistake of your life was letting her go. Again, another bad idea. He'd been the one to break it off with her.

"Hi, Zeke," she said softly.

"Hey," he said. That sounded dumb.

"I was wondering when you would get here."

He stiffened. "You were expecting me?"

She leaned against the door, her hand still grasping the knob. "I hope you don't mind. I asked for Grace's help. I didn't know how she'd do it, but she assured me she would get you out here."

"Actually, it was Brielle..." He sighed as the realization hit him. Of course they all knew. There were no secrets when it came to his family. At least there were no secrets between his daughters. They all knew about him and his dirty laundry.

"Brielle said she wanted me to check on the cabin and make sure it was in good shape so she could stay here with Wade."

Agatha covered her mouth, but it did nothing to hide the smile she wore. "Sorry. I didn't mean to drag your children into a lie."

He shifted his weight from one foot to the other and smiled back. "I'm sure it was the highlight of their week. My kids have been interested in what I'm up to these days more than their own lives."

Her soft smile drew him like a moth to the flame. Even though her face was emblazoned in his mind, he'd managed to forget just what it was like to be graced by her presence. She could make him feel like he was the only man in the world, and all it took was the corners of her lips lifting in just the right way.

"Thomas came by the other day. We had a long talk."

"Oh?"

She nodded. "I don't suppose you would have anything to do with that, would you?"

This was a test. It had to be. If he told her he was the reason her son was finally opening up, she could blame him for controlling her life again. He wasn't about to slip up now, not when he was enjoying her company so much. "I guess that would depend."

"Depend on what?" she said softly.

"On how it worked out between you and your son."

She tilted her head, her eyes full of joy. He hadn't seen her so happy since before Thomas had told his lie. This was a side of her that only solidified the realization of what exactly he'd lost. "Thank you," she whispered.

"Thank you? You're not going to tell me that I meddled and that I need to stop being so controlling?"

The grin told him all he needed to know. "Then, in that case, I might have had a discussion with your son on the importance of communication."

Agatha jerked her chin over her shoulder. "Would you like to come in for some lunch? I made grilled cheese."

"Well, if it's grilled cheese, then how can I refuse?" He moved forward, and she stepped back to give him entrance. The cabin looked exactly as he'd left it but with one small difference. The kitchen table had been set with two plates, two cups, silverware, and a vase of flowers. He glanced at her and chuckled. "What if I hadn't shown up?"

She shrugged. "I guess we'll never know, will we?"

Being with her in his cabin like this brought back so many memories of their shared breakfasts together. It was funny how he suddenly couldn't even recall the reasons he'd broken things off with her—something to do with them not being compatible.

Agatha hurried over to the stove area and retrieved a platter with two sandwiches and two small bowls of soup. She returned to place them at their seats and her eyes met his. "I hope you like tomato. It's the only thing I eat with grilled cheese."

"Sounds great." Zeke pulled out her chair and motioned for her to take a seat.

Once they faced each other, he picked up his sandwich and took a bite. A moan of contentment slipped through his lips, and he nodded toward her. "This has got to be the best grilled cheese sandwich I have ever had."

She laughed. "Don't be ridiculous. This was merely a way to get you inside so we could talk."

"Uh-oh. I don't know if I like the sound of that."

In all seriousness, she said, "Perhaps you won't."

He put down his sandwich and wiped his mouth. "Well then, I suppose we should get started."

She dipped her gaze down to his sandwich and then back to his face. "Well, I want you to enjoy your meal. No sense in it getting cold."

"Agatha, I assume you wanted me to come out here so we

could have a frank discussion. I also assume that you have likely gone over what it is you want to say several times until you've got it right. Would I be correct in these assumptions?" He'd learned a lot over the past weeks about himself and the woman he had come to have feelings for—mostly as he tried to dissect what he could have done differently. And the biggest thing he'd found out was that he jumped in too fast without allowing her to say her piece. Agatha was the kind of woman who needed to feel heard. This was his way of giving her what she needed. And when she was all done, he'd take advantage of this situation and tell her exactly what he thought of her—how much he missed her and that letting her go was the biggest mistake of his life.

Agatha cleared her throat and nodded. "You're right. I wanted you here for a reason. I've had an epiphany of sorts." She let out a soft laugh and looked away. "This is going to be a little embarrassing, but I've realized that I've been prioritizing everything wrong."

He didn't know what to say. What could she possibly be referring to?

She chuckled nervously again. "When Thomas was born, he was my whole world. He became my identity. And as he continued to grow up, I kept that relationship exactly the way it was without allowing him to advance and move on. I had to be independent so I could take care of both of us. It was a mechanism for me to keep us safe. I couldn't depend on anyone else for both of our sakes."

"That's understandable," Zeke said. "You had to protect your family."

"Yes, but when I moved out here, things didn't change. I was still trying to fulfill that role, and in doing so, I wasn't letting you in. I wasn't allowing you to take care of me."

He straightened, finally comprehending where she was going with all of this.

"Letting go has got to be one of the hardest things I've ever had to do in my entire life." This time she let her gaze lock onto his, sending a shiver coursing through his body. "You might think it's for the best that we part ways, but you couldn't be more wrong. This isn't about you. And it's not about me. It's about both of us, and as such, we both get a say in what happens."

She couldn't be saying what he thought she was saying, could she? His heart flickered to life as if it hadn't been awake since the last time he'd held her in his arms. This was more than he could have ever hoped to happen. "Agatha, I want—"

"No, let me finish. If you think that breaking up is the smart thing to do without even a thought to how we could work this out, then I need to ask you to take another hard look at what you want. You either want me or you don't." She took a deep breath and blew it out hard before she continued speaking. "I have already thought about this from every angle. I can see every outcome from this meeting, and if I had my way, I'd say there isn't a second option. We're going to approach this like we have nothing to lose. This relationship isn't about my son or your daughters. It isn't about your irritating need to be some kind of knight in shining armor, nor is it about my debilitating need to make sure I'm independent and taking care of things the way I think is best. This is about *us*. This is about how you make me happy, and I don't care what it takes. I'm going to fight for it."

Zeke peered at her, loving how she squirmed and fidgeted after giving her speech. Apparently, he hadn't lost his touch after all. He'd managed to make her nervous just like everyone else in town. "Are you finished?" he finally said.

She nodded.

"Well, I must say that all of this is fairly unexpected. I mean, first, you ambush me at *my* cabin. Then expect me to sit at *my* table eating food I'm assuming came from *my* refrigerator."

"Actually, it—"

"Agatha," he said softly. "I don't care how it happened. I'm just glad it did." He reached across the table and grasped her hand in his. "I understand what makes you tick. I get that people have failed you in the past. But that's not going to be me. I'm done making excuses. I'm tired of being in a position where I feel like I have to control every outcome. But if you're on my side, I know I can take whatever life throws at me—at *us*," he corrected.

She squeezed his hand. "I don't know how to explain it, but I feel… whole when I'm with you."

"Even when I boss you around?"

Agatha laughed. "Well, I think we're going to have to work on that."

He shook his head, making a clicking sound. "Nope. I'm a package deal. You get what you see."

She made a face, and he laughed.

"Okay, fine." Zeke lifted up his sandwich and took a large bite. After he swallowed, he waved it back and forth. "If you keep making food like this, I think I can be convinced to tone it down… just a little bit."

"Deal." She stood up and leaned over her plate, then he did the same. They shared a kiss, one full of promises—promises of mistakes, promises of compromise, and promises of grilled cheese sandwiches.

EPILOGUE

Six Months Later

Agatha

Agatha wrung her hands as she paced her kitchen. "Are you sure they will want to come? I mean, it's different for me to visit when one of your daughters is hosting, but—"

Zeke took both of her hands in his. "It's going to be *fine*. It's not like they're unaware of how serious it is between us. In fact, I'm pretty sure I heard Brielle ask when we were going to get hitched."

Agatha shot him a surprised look. Marriage? She'd be lying to herself if she said she hadn't considered it. But she also didn't know if it was something Zeke wanted. She'd figured she'd wait until he brought it up first.

Funny how this was the first time in her life that she had zero interest in taking control. The thought of even bringing it up filled her with a mixture of excitement and dread. That couldn't be healthy, could it?

Zeke moved closer to her, his eyes searching hers. It was as if he wanted a sign she was ready. Or maybe he was just testing the waters and wanted to make sure she was in the same place as him... a place that wasn't even thinking about tying the knot.

Agatha let out a quiet, anxious laugh. "What?"

"Are you okay?"

"Of course I am." She moved to get away from him, but his hands still held hers too tightly.

"Agatha."

"What?"

He tilted his head and a small smile touched his lips. "What are you thinking?"

Another laugh. Why did she have to react that way when he was around her? Agatha squeezed his hands and glanced away. "I'm just nervous. That's all. I want them to like coming here. I want them to see me as someone they can spend time with. Ever since Thomas moved to Colorado Springs..." She let out a heavy sigh. "It's just not the same." She almost said she felt so alone, but she couldn't bring herself to do so when the one person who made her life beautiful was standing in front of her.

"You miss him."

"Of course I miss him. He's my only child. I've never lived this far away from him before and even a few hours seems like millions of miles." Agatha blinked back the tears that came more often than not when she talked about her son. "He's happy. So I'm happy. But... like I said... it's not the same."

Zeke released her hands and pulled her in for a tight hug. "I get it," he whispered. "Change is hard. It's scary. And it's definitely something that is only made easier when you have someone to help carry that burden."

"I suppose you're right," she murmured into his shoulder. "If it weren't for you, I don't know that I would have been able to handle staying here."

"Oh, I don't know about that," Zeke teased. He pulled away and tucked a strand of hair behind her ear. "You have Shane and the folks at the club you work with. You have that horse... what did you name her?"

"Henrietta." She chuckled. "And thank you. It was very generous of you to give her to me."

"Well, it was either Henrietta or an ATV. I wasn't about to go a single day without seeing you, and sometimes it's just easier to meet in the middle."

She leaned into him, allowing his warmth to wash over her. Everything hadn't been perfect by any stretch of the imagination. The two of them still butted heads every so often, but in the end, they found ways to compromise.

Agatha had found a new purpose at work as well. She'd pulled Shane aside and asked him his thoughts on setting up a summer program for at-risk teens. He seemed to like the concept, and they were going to have a meeting about it in about a week.

If Agatha could be the one to head the project, she felt she could truly find her purpose again. Raising her son had been the highlight of her life and a calling she'd been proud to have.

"... and that's why I think we needed to talk about it before they arrive."

Agatha jumped and pulled away just enough to get a good view of Zeke's eyes. "I'm so sorry. What were you saying?"

He got a funny look on his face. "You're not going to make me say it again, are you?"

She scrunched up her face, tilting her head to the side as she gave him an apologetic smile. "I got lost in my thoughts again. I really think that the summer program could do so much good for the kids who grow up without much purpose."

Zeke shook his head, but he didn't appear upset at all. "That's why I love you. You're always wanting something more —but not in a bad way. You're not the type to sit back and let the world pass you by. I'd guess that when you're eighty-two, you'll still be living out in the country telling the cowboys what they're doing wrong."

"Cowboys?" she laughed. "What cowboys? When I'm eighty-two, I plan on living the high life in a condo in the city."

Zeke's expression faltered. "You want to move to the city?"

This time it was her turn to laugh. "Of course not." Agatha wrapped her arms around his neck and leaned in close to press a soft kiss to his cheek. "Honestly? I think I'd be happy anywhere as long as I'm with you."

The look he gave her made her stomach flip over on its side and her pulse raced faster than a rocket to the moon. "Is that so?" he said.

Agatha nodded. "I love you, Zeke Callahan."

"Prove it," he whispered.

"Anything," she responded.

"Marry me."

Every part of her body ran cold, then hot. Her face flushed and her eyes grew wide. "So you weren't just saying that. Earlier, when you said…"

"I wasn't just saying anything. I think Brielle has a point. We love each other. We're definitely not getting any younger, so why wait?"

"Why… wait?" Agatha said breathily. "What are you saying?"

"I'm saying I don't have to have some big fancy wedding. I just want to call you mine. I want to spend the rest of my life knowing I won the heart of the amazing Agatha Birch." Zeke lowered down onto one knee and withdrew a small red velvet box.

Agatha gasped.

"Will you do me the honor of becoming my wife? I know our lives won't be easy. You'd be taking on a lot of daughters… and their husbands… and subsequent grandchildren—"

She pressed a finger to his lips. "Yes! You had me at grand-children."

He chuckled, but before he could respond, the front door to the house opened. "Anyone home? Hope you don't mind that we let ourselves in." Brielle and Wade were the first to arrive in the doorway that led to the kitchen, and they found Zeke still on one knee, Agatha's hand in his.

Brielle gasped, her eyes bouncing from her father to Agatha and back. "Oh my goodness! Please tell me you put him out of his misery and told him yes."

"Bri, just let them tell their story," Wade muttered. He lifted a bag. "I brought the chips like you asked. But if you're in the middle of something, we can—"

"Oh, don't be ridiculous." She wiped just below her eyes with her fingers and let out a laugh. "You're right on time."

"Well?" Brielle exclaimed. "Don't leave us hanging. What's going to happen? Are we adding another Callahan to the lineup?"

"Another?" Zeke groaned as he got to his feet. "Thanks to all my daughters, there won't be any more Callahans. You saw to it when you all got married."

Brielle glanced at Wade, a small smile touching her lips.

Wade held up both hands. "I told her she didn't have to change her name, but she's insisting she wants to be a Keagan."

Zeke huffed. "Like there aren't enough already? I think the world could do with a few less."

Agatha pushed his shoulder. "Zeke, how could you say such a thing?"

He gestured toward Wade, his expression still serious. "Have you heard about his family? It's the largest one in the area. You wanna talk numbers? How many is it, Wade? Ten children?"

"Ten boys," Brielle offered. "But he has two sisters, too."

Agatha's mouth fell open. "Twelve children? How did you

even manage..." She'd thought raising one son on her own had been hard. And she'd heard the stories of the Keagan children practically raising themselves, but she'd never heard just how large their family truly was.

Wade chuckled. "It's not so bad. There are a lot of us, sure, but we're a tight-knit group. We have to be. If we didn't stick our necks out for each other, who would?" He glanced down at Brielle, and that glowing smile was enough to make Agatha realize just what she'd been missing all of these years.

Feeling Zeke's eyes on her, she met his gaze with a loving one of her own. She turned back to Wade. "Are all of your siblings married?"

Wade let out a raucous laugh. "Not on your life. I'm the oldest, so I was basically setting the example for the rest of them. Then my sister... well, she's not really interested in getting tied down."

"Sounds familiar," Zeke said as he eyed Brielle, who only grinned at him.

"I guess the most likely one of us to settle down next would be Elijah. He's more down to earth and probably more willing to make the sacrifices necessary to find a wife."

Brielle nudged Wade in the side. "What about Lucas? He's kinda a ladies' man, isn't he? I swear I see him with a different girl every other week. Who's to say that he wouldn't be the next to find that special someone who could convince him to tie the knot?"

"Lucas?" Wade shook his head and laughed. "There's not a woman strong enough to wrangle him. He's having too much fun right now. It's hard enough as it is to get him to do the work that needs to get done at the ranch, let alone get serious about a girl. Nope, I don't think he'll ever find anyone. And if he does, it's not going to be any time soon."

Agatha smiled. "Well, you never know. Sometimes the right person just comes along and you're powerless to control it."

Agatha glanced lovingly at the man who'd done just that. He slipped his arm around her waist, and she snuggled closer to him.

Zeke nodded. "Truer words have never been spoken."

OKAY READER... this wraps it up for the Callahans! I hope you enjoyed Zeke and Agatha's later in life love story.

THE CALLAHANS' stories may be complete, but the neighboring ranch has its own set of cowboys and heart-tugging tales to tell.

MEET the Keagans of Copper Creek—where rugged cowboys, strong women, and deep family ties take center stage. From forbidden love to second chances, these stories are filled with faith, redemption, and happily-ever-afters.

DON'T MISS the start of this beloved new series—*Some Cowboys Are Off-Limits, Keagans of Copper Creek Book 1.* I think you'll love seeing Elijah Keagan fall for his sister's best friend! Look for the paperback at **nataliedeanbooks.com** and other retailers.

ABOUT THE AUTHOR

Born and raised in a small coastal town in the south, I was raised to treasure family and love the Lord. I'm a dedicated homeschooling mom who loves to travel and spend time with my growing-up-too-fast son.

When I'm not busy writing or running my business, you can find me cleaning house, cooking dinner, feeding our three rescue cats, trying to make learning fun and coaxing my son to pick up his toys. On less busy days, you may also find me paddling down a spring run in Florida, hiking a mountain trail in Georgia (on the rare vacation to the mountains), or enjoying a book.

If you love Natalie Dean books, you can be notified of new

releases by signing up to my newsletter at nataliedeanau thor.com, where you will also receive two free short stories for signing up. Just click on the "Free Books" tab at the top and you'll be on your way!

Also, as previously mentioned, I've opened my own online bookstore and I'd love your support! As of June 2024, I'm selling my ebooks at Natalie Dean Books. By late summer or fall 2024, I should have audiobooks, regular paperbacks, large print paperbacks, dyslexic print paperbacks and signed paperbacks all available. At the request of my loyal readers, I'll also be adding merchandise, such as glasses, cups, magnets and more. So come check out my small mom-owned author business at nataliedeanbooks.com.

You can also scan the QR code below to be taken to the home page of Natalie Dean Books.

facebook.com/nataliedeanromance

www.ingramcontent.com/pod-product-compliance
Lightning Source LLC
Chambersburg PA
CBHW020145310726
48970CB00006B/2018